SHOWDOWN

"I was wondering if you'd like to go out sometime this week," Jack proposed. "How does the day after tomorrow sound?"

Wednesday, Jessica thought. That was two days before Lila would even have a chance at him. "Wednesday's perfect."

"So, I'll see you then. I'm looking forward to it," Jack said.

"Me, too," replied Jessica. After she said goodbye, she put down the receiver and gave a shriek of excitement.

"Jess, what are you yelling about?" Mrs. Wakefield called from the other room.

"Oh, nothing, Mom," she called back. *Nothing except the most gorgeous, charming, mysteriously exciting guy in the whole world,* she added to herself. Let Lila sneak behind her father's back. Jessica was convinced that she wouldn't be doing it for long. Because soon Jack would be eating out of Jessica's hand, and Lila would be nothing more than a name in his past.

Bantam Books in the Sweet Valley High Series
Ask your bookseller for the books you have missed

SWEET VALLEY HIGH

SHOWDOWN

Written by
Kate William

Created by
FRANCINE PASCAL

BANTAM BOOKS
TORONTO · NEW YORK · LONDON · SYDNEY · AUCKLAND

RL 6, IL age 12 and up

SHOWDOWN
A Bantam Book / May 1985

Sweet Valley High is a trademark of Francine Pascal

Conceived by Francine Pascal

Produced by Cloverdale Press Inc.,
133 Fifth Avenue, New York, N.Y. 10003

Cover art by James Mathewuse

ISBN 0-553-24893-6

Published simultaneously in the United States and Canada

PRINTED IN THE UNITED STATES OF AMERICA

O   0 9 8 7 6 5 4 3 2 1

SHOWDOWN

One

"I just can't wait to meet Lila's mystery man," Jessica Wakefield announced to her twin sister as they cleaned up after their usual Sunday family brunch. Her blue-green eyes sparkled with excitement. "The guy sounds unbelievable." She carried a stack of dishes from the table to the kitchen counter.

"Well, I'm sure you'll have plenty of time to get a look at him this afternoon," Elizabeth remarked, scraping the plates and then carefully loading them into the dishwasher. "Knowing Lila Fowler, she probably invented this whole pool party just to lure him over to her house and show him off to everyone." She laughed good-naturedly.

"Not to mention showing Fowler Crest to him, in all its splendor," Jessica added, referring to the sprawling estate where her friend Lila lived. "I swear, Lila never gets tired of flaunting her wealth." There was disdain in her voice,

1

although Elizabeth thought she detected a note of envy as well.

"Whatever the case," Elizabeth commented, "Lila sure picked a perfect day for an outdoor party. It should be great." The morning sun poured through the wide-open windows into the Wakefields' Spanish-tiled kitchen.

"Especially if this guy Jack is as fabulous as Lila's made him out to be," Jessica added.

Elizabeth gave her sister a hard stare. "Jessica Wakefield. You're *not*, by any strange chance, thinking of going after Lila's new friend yourself."

"I'm not?" Jessica asked with mock innocence. "And why not, if he's so fabulous?"

"Honestly, Jess." Elizabeth shook her head in disbelief, her sun-streaked blond hair glinting in the sunlight. "You haven't even met the guy yet."

"So? The one thing I've got to say for Lila is that she usually has terrific taste. And from the way she's been raving about Jack, he must be hotter than all the guys at Sweet Valley High put together."

"But what about Lila?" Elizabeth finished loading the dishwasher and tackled the greasy frying pan and dirty pot in the sink. "She's your friend, and she met him first."

"And I'll meet him next." Jessica hoisted herself up onto the kitchen counter and watched her sister work.

2

Elizabeth sighed. Sometimes it was just useless to try to reason with her twin. Jessica was only four minutes younger than she was, but at times like this, Elizabeth felt as if it were more like four years. Identical on the outside, from their perfect size-six figures to their shoulder-length blond hair and brilliant smiles, the girls were as different on the inside as two sixteen-year-olds could be.

Jessica liked being at the center of the action, and there was no trick she didn't know about getting there—and staying there. You could often find Elizabeth alone, on the other hand, hard at work on her latest assignment for the Sweet Valley High newspaper, *The Oracle*. Or you could find her sharing a quiet evening with her steady boyfriend, Todd Wilkins, or her best friend, Enid Rollins.

But right now Elizabeth's attention was focused on her twin. "And what about Neil Freemount?" she asked.

"Neil? He and I are just good friends," Jessica replied. "I mean, sure, he's taking me to this party, but he doesn't mind if I spend time with other guys. Just like I don't mind if he hangs around with other girls."

"He never does, Jess," Elizabeth said sternly.

Jessica shrugged. "That's not my problem. You know, Liz"—she gave a little laugh—"I can't help it if I drive boys wild."

Elizabeth tried hard to keep a straight face, but

a giggle finally escaped her lips. "OK, OK, Jess—you win. You're charming and irresistible."

Jessica grinned. "Don't stop, Liz."

Elizabeth burst out laughing. "All right. And clever, and a good dancer. And the best cheerleader Sweet Valley High has ever had. Oh—and, of course, absolutely gorgeous."

"Of course." Jessica nodded her head vigorously.

"But you're also going to be a dead duck if you don't pick up a dish towel and start drying these pots and pans. And then you'll never get to meet the famed Jack."

"Well, we can't have that, can we?" Jessica gave her twin a little salute, jumped off the counter, and got to work.

Elizabeth climbed out of the pool and stretched her lithe, tanned body out on a large beach towel next to her boyfriend, Todd Wilkins. To one side of them lay the sprawling Fowler mansion with its Spanish-style patio; to the other, a broad expanse of perfectly landscaped lawn and gardens and a spectacular view of the town of Sweet Valley, nestled far below.

"Great view from up here, huh?" Todd commented.

Elizabeth nodded, scanning the lush California landscape.

Todd rolled over on his side so he was facing his girlfriend. "But I've got a better view right

4

now." He took one of Elizabeth's hands in his and gave her that wonderful smile that never failed to make her heart skip a beat.

"You're not so bad yourself," Elizabeth returned teasingly, taking in Todd's lean, muscular build, his warm brown eyes, and the shock of dark hair that fell over his forehead. She reached over and gave him a tender kiss.

"Hey—what's all this about?" a girl's voice called playfully. Elizabeth looked up to see her best friend, Enid Rollins, coming across the lawn with her boyfriend, George Warren, a freshman at nearby Sweet Valley College.

"Oops, caught in the act." Elizabeth smiled as Enid and George spread their towels next to her and Todd. "Where have you guys been, anyway? I thought maybe you'd decided not to come."

"George had a flying lesson," Enid explained. "And I went out to the airfield to pick him up when it was over."

"Oh, that's right." Elizabeth nodded. "I forgot—today's a flying day. How's that going, George?"

George grinned. "It's fantastic. You can't imagine how it feels to be soaring through the air in the cockpit of your own glider." He looked up at the bright, cloudless sky as if to emphasize his point.

"That's what my friend Robin Wilson's been

telling me," Elizabeth said. "She's taking the same course."

"Robin? She's one of the best students in the program," George commented.

"Except for you," Enid joked, her green eyes twinkling.

"Well, what else would you expect?" George kidded back, giving his girlfriend an affectionate swat on the arm.

"So, Mr. Super Flyer, when do you take the test for your pilot's license?" Todd asked.

"Two weeks from yesterday," George answered. "And you and Liz will be the first people I give a ride to, after Enid."

Suddenly, loud laughter erupted from the direction of the pool. The four friends turned to see tall, lanky Winston Egbert, the clown of the Sweet Valley High junior class, challenging handsome Nicholas Morrow to a dog-paddle race across the pool. Elizabeth giggled as Winston and Nicholas fought to pull themselves through the water, their arms paddling frantically while they strained to keep their heads above it.

The amusement of the onlookers was contagious, and soon Winston and Nicholas were laughing as hard as anyone else, spurting water out of their mouths as they struggled across to the deep end of the pool and back. The kids standing around the pool cheered noisily as Nicholas and Winston touched the edge at the same moment.

Elsewhere on the grounds of Fowler Crest, a badminton game was in full swing, while nearby, Olivia Davidson, the arts editor for *The Oracle*, strummed her guitar, a group of people singing along with her.

"Great party," Enid observed.

"Except for one thing." Elizabeth turned toward a grove of palm trees at the side of the huge house. Under it, Lila Fowler sat alone. "Lila's mystery guest hasn't arrived yet." *And Lila's not the only one who's wondering where he is*, Elizabeth thought to herself. Jessica had spent the better part of the afternoon surrounded by her faithful fans—Cara Walker, her best friend; Neil Freemount; and several other admirers. But whenever she thought no one was looking, she would glance over her shoulder to see if anyone new had arrived. To most of the guests at the party, it looked as if Jessica was having a fabulous time. But her twin sister wasn't fooled; Elizabeth knew Jessica was disappointed.

"Gee, that's too bad," Enid said. "I was getting kind of curious about Lila's date, myself. I mean Lila doesn't go out of her way like this for just anybody." She motioned to the buffet table set up on the patio. Trays were piled high with fresh berries, grapes, cherries, and pieces of melon and pineapple. Delicate cakes and pastries were arranged on the table, too, along with imported cheeses, several different kinds of crackers, cold cuts, chips, raw vegetables, and a number of dips. A red- and white-striped canopy was set up over the feast to keep it out of the sun. Elizabeth watched as surfer Bill Chase and his girlfriend, DeeDee Gordon, piled their plates high with food.

"It does look like a great spread," said Todd, eyeing the buffet hungrily. "Should we go sample it?"

"You bet!" George answered, and the two couples got up and headed for the buffet table.

Elizabeth was trying to decide between an apple turnover and a cinnamon-raisin swirl when Lila's voice floated across the grass.

"Oh, Jack," she gushed, "I'm so glad you made it. The afternoon just wouldn't have been a success without you." Elizabeth turned and watched Lila join the party with a tall, well-built young man. His powerful-looking arms and handsome face were deeply tanned, and his honey-brown hair was shot with sun-lightened streaks. He was dressed conservatively in a pair of khaki walking shorts, a green Lacoste shirt, and Top-Siders.

So he finally got here, Elizabeth thought to herself. Jessica would be happy.

"Oh, boy," declared Cara Walker, who had come up beside Elizabeth at the refreshment table. "Lila wasn't kidding when she said he was gorgeous." Her gaze followed Jack as he and Lila approached the pool.

Jessica, seated next to Neil on the Fowlers'

8

lawn, also noted Jack's arrival. *Wow!* she thought to herself. *Before I was only half-serious about stealing him from Lila. But now* . . . She watched the good-looking boy's every move as he was introduced to some of the kids around the pool. "Neil," Jessica said, "I don't know about you, but I'm broiling. I think I'll go take a swim." And without waiting for a response, Jessica was up in a flash, heading for the pool—and Jack. When she got within a few feet of him and had made sure he was looking in her direction, she slipped out of her terry-cloth beach robe, revealing a minuscule turquoise bikini that showed off her every curve. She mounted the diving board and, without a second's hesitation, executed a graceful backflip into the water.

"Nice dive," Jack remarked to Lila.

"Umm," Lila replied noncommittally.

A second later Jessica surfaced. She looked over at Lila and Jack, and waved. "Come on in. The water's great." She smiled brightly.

"It does look good," she heard Jack say to Lila. "Shall we?"

"I guess so," Lila muttered, sounding unenthusiastic about having to share Jack's attention. "You can change into your suit over there." She pointed to a small cabana near the shallow end of the pool.

As Jack walked off, Jessica eyed Lila carefully. Her light brown hair was swept up off her face in a becoming French braid. Her shiny black bikini was as skimpy as Jessica's. And Lila's trim figure was almost as good. Almost, Jessica noted. Jessica shifted her focus as Jack emerged from the cabana in a navy-blue racing suit. *Omigod*, she thought, *the less this guy wears, the better he looks!*

She watched Lila join Jack at the edge of the pool and gingerly dip her toe in the water.

"After you," Jack said gallantly to his hostess.

Lila lowered herself into the pool, and Jack dived in after her. When he came up, Jessica was at his side.

"Hi," she said, flashing him a blinding grin. "I don't believe we've been introduced."

Without missing a beat, Lila swam over to Jessica and Jack and positioned herself directly between the two of them. "This is my dear friend Jessica Wakefield," she said as she treaded water. Lila turned her back to Jack for a split second and shot Jessica a look of purest ice. Then she looked at Jack again and smiled sweetly. "And, Jess, this is my new friend, Jack."

"Nice to meet you, Jessica," he said in a friendly voice.

"Likewise," Jessica responded, swimming around so she was next to him again.

As if in a water-bound game of musical chairs, Lila swam between the two of them again and faced Jack. "How about a few laps across the pool?" she asked, trying to ease Jessica out of the picture.

10

"OK," Jack agreed amicably.

Lila flipped onto her back and made a few paddling motions. "Later, Jess," she said pointedly.

"See you soon," Jack told her.

"You can count on it," Jessica responded, refusing to be daunted by Lila's "hands-off" signals. She watched them swim across the pool, noting Jack's strong, smooth strokes as he glided through the water. Every few yards he would stop and wait for Lila to catch up with him. *He's a real gentleman*, Jessica thought. *Definitely the kind of guy who interests me.* Now all she had to do was to get him alone.

That proved more difficult than Jessica had imagined. Lila didn't let Jack out of her sight for even a minute, shepherding him from one group of friends to another, her arm linked through his. Jack seemed to charm everybody. He was very polite, but not at all stuffy. He took an interest in each person he met, and though he obviously had a lot to envy, he never once boasted. In fact, he barely said a word about himself. Though he was clearly the center of attention, he remained a mystery—a mystery that, as the party wore on, Jessica became more and more eager to unravel.

But as the day wore on, Jessica still hadn't found a chance to talk to Jack again, until she spotted Lila introducing him to Elizabeth, Todd,

Nicholas Morrow, and Aaron Dallas near the badminton court. "Excuse me," Jessica said to Ken Matthews, who had been telling her about a new stunt he'd learned to do on water skis. "I just remembered something I have to tell my sister." Seizing her opportunity, she sprinted over to the group just in time to catch the end of Jack's sentence.

". . . but I thought you had on a different bathing suit earlier," he was saying to Elizabeth, who was wearing a simple, off-white tank suit.

Jessica came up and wrapped her arm around her twin's shoulders, watching Jack's confused expression turn to one of understanding.

"Oh, I see. Twins." Jack chuckled.

Elizabeth extended her hand. "I'm Liz," she said.

"A pleasure to meet you. My name's Jack."

"And this is Todd and Aaron," Elizabeth introduced them. "And Nicholas."

Nicholas eyed Jack curiously as the two boys shook hands. "Jack, you look so familiar," he observed. "Do we know each other from someplace?"

For the first time since he'd arrived, Jack appeared to be a bit flustered. "No. I—ah—can't imagine where we could have met before," he stammered.

"Sailing camp?" Nicholas questioned. "I used to go to Teela Locca sailing camp in New Hampshire when I was a kid." Jack shook his head.

"Hmm. Well, what about Martha's Vineyard? My family used to have a summer house there."

"Nope," Jack said, shifting from one foot to the other. Jessica thought he looked decidedly uncomfortable, and she wondered why.

"You've never spent any time on the East Coast?" Nicholas persisted. "My family recently moved from there."

Jack studied the ground. "I've been there," he mumbled, "but I really can't remember ever seeing you before."

"Maybe you know my sister, Regina Morrow."

Nicholas's sister, a classmate of the twins, had been deaf from birth. She was now at a special clinic in Switzerland, undergoing a series of operations to correct her handicap.

"The name doesn't sound familiar." Jack shook his head.

"Oh, well," Nicholas said. "Maybe you just look like somebody I know." But he didn't sound convinced. "Anyway"—he waved his hand—"we were just about to play a game of badminton. Would you two care to join us?"

Lila spoke up hastily. "No, I wanted to show Jack the new gym my father's installing."

It was plain to Jessica that Lila wanted to spend some time alone with Jack before the party wound down. A number of the guests had already said goodbye, so this was her last chance. But Jessica had every intention of spending the end of the party with Jack as well, and she didn't plan to let Lila stop her. "Oh, I'd love to see the gym, too," Jessica invited herself along.

Lila appeared distressed, but clearly there was nothing she could do. Squaring her shoulders, she led Jack and Jessica inside the enormous house. As they walked into the foyer, decorated with a huge abstract painting—something outrageously expensive, Jessica was certain—they heard the faint ringing of the phone.

Lila pouted. "Oh, no. And it's the servants' day off, too. I guess I have to answer that." She looked from Jack to Jessica, biting down hard on her lower lip as she studied Jessica's gleeful expression. Finally Lila gave an exasperated sigh and dashed off to answer the call.

Now was Jessica's big chance. "So," she said, moving as close to Jack as she could without actually touching him. "I don't think I've ever seen you around town before. I mean, I'd certainly remember you if I had." Her voice was as sweet as maple syrup. "Have you just moved to Sweet Valley?"

"I've been here for a few months," Jack replied pleasantly.

"Do you go to school around here?" Jessica queried.

"No, I'm taking some time off between high school and college. I want a chance to be on my own," he explained. "But let's talk about you. Tell me about yourself."

Jessica was happy to oblige. She told him about being co-captain of the Sweet Valley High cheerleaders; she told him a little about her parents—Mr. Wakefield, a prominent lawyer, and Mrs. Wakefield, an interior designer. "I have a brother, Steven, who's a college freshman," Jessica finished, "and you've already met my twin sister, Liz."

Jack nodded. "The prettiest twins I've ever seen."

Jessica felt her pulse race. Jack was definitely interested in her. He had to be. "Listen," she said suddenly. "I'd love a chance to get to know you better."

Jack smiled.

"Why don't you give me a call sometime, and we can have dinner together or something," Jessica continued. She let her voice linger suggestively on the "or something."

"Sounds great," Jack agreed.

Jessica allowed herself a triumphant smile. "I'm sure we'll have a great time," she said. "Here, let me give you my phone number."

She looked around for a pen or pencil, but there was nothing on the little steel and glass table in the foyer except a small book of matches. Quickly she picked up the matches, struck one, and then blew it out. She used the charred tip to write her number on the inside of the matchbook cover. "There you go." She pressed the match-book into Jack's hand and let their fingers touch for a moment.

As the electricity flowed between them, Jessica heard Lila returning. She pulled her hand back and took a step away from Jack. "You were just about to tell me what it is you're doing in Sweet Valley," she said innocently, as Lila entered the foyer.

"I was?" Jack looked vaguely amused.

"Maybe you *should* tell her, Jack." Lila came over and put a possessive hand on his shoulder. "You're going to have to spill the beans about yourself sooner or later."

"That's true," responded Jack.

Here it comes, thought Jessica. *He's a famous actor, but nobody could quite place the face. Or better yet, he's terribly rich, and he doesn't have to work at all. Maybe he's even nobility. Exactly the kind of guy I want the world to see me with.*

Jack turned toward Jessica. "The truth of the matter, Jess"—he took a deep breath—"is that I'm a construction worker."

Two

Lila lay stretched out on a deck chair by the side of the pool. She sipped iced tea as the sun began to dip behind the mountains surrounding Sweet Valley and the sky turned a fiery red. Jack was beside her; all the other guests had left.

She had managed to keep Jack away from Jessica for the rest of the party. Or rather, Jessica had pretty much stayed away on her own, darting occasional glances in Jack's direction as if she couldn't decide whether or not she ought to be seen with a mere construction worker. Jessica had always thought that only the richest guys, the most popular, and the privileged were good enough for her, and usually Lila was of one mind with her about that. But Lila was convinced that Jack was no ordinary construction worker. His wardrobe, his bearing, his entire manner were princely. There had to be more to him than he was letting on.

Jessica seemed to have reached the same conclusion by the time the party was over. "Lila," she'd whispered to her hostess as she was leaving with Neil Freemount and while Jack was inside the house, making a phone call, "you don't think he's really a manual laborer—I mean underneath it all."

Lila had shrugged noncommittally. "Maybe we just have to believe what he says." She didn't let on that she agreed with Jessica, or that she suspected there was something about Jack's background that he was keeping secret. But now was the time to discover what that something was.

Lila inched her deck chair closer to Jack's. "So, what were you doing before you came to Sweet Valley?" she asked casually, gazing at his classic profile outlined against the darkening sky.

"More construction," Jack replied. "In another town."

Lila was silent for a couple of moments. "It's funny," she said. "Even though I've seen you at work, seen you lifting and hammering and stuff, you don't really seem like the construction-worker type. Not that there's anything wrong with doing construction work," she added quickly. She didn't want to risk offending him.

"So what type do you think I am?" Jack questioned.

"Well . . ." Lila took a long, slow sip of her iced tea. "You seem somehow—I don't know—more important, like you're destined for big things. . . ." She groped for words.

18

"And you don't think building buildings and fixing water mains and paving roads is important?" Jack asked. Nevertheless, he looked pleased by Lila's observation.

"That's—that's not what I meant. It's—well . . ." Lila's voice trailed off.

"I know what you mean," Jack volunteered. "I was really only teasing you. I'm actually very flattered."

"But you are a full-time construction worker?" she asked.

Lila's first reaction was one of extreme disappointment. With his nod, her balloon of happiness had been deflated. Her second reaction was one of relief, relief that her father hadn't been able to get back from his business trip before the end of the party. It was he who had called earlier, to say that his plane had been delayed and that he'd be home a day later than he'd expected. Lila had been a bit upset. She spent little enough time with her father as it was. But now she was glad. No matter how unusual Jack was for a construction worker, she knew her father would never approve of him. Not even as just a date for a party.

"But, Lila," Jack's words cut into Lila's glum thoughts, "my life hasn't been anything like the rest of the guys I work with."

"It hasn't?" Lila asked. A glimmer of hope surfaced in a gloomy sea.

"No. Lila, can you keep a secret?"

"Of course!" Lila exclaimed. She'd been right! Jack was hiding something important about himself. And she was on the verge of finding out what it was!

"You promise not to tell a soul?" Jack insisted. Lila nodded eagerly.

"I left home almost a year ago." Jack drained the last bit of iced tea left in his glass. "My father is a very important and powerful man and is used to running everyone's life. Including mine. He sent me to the 'right' summer camp, the 'right' prep school, and was planning on sending me off to Princeton—just like him and my grandfather before him. He had my whole life mapped out already. And I was just supposed to be some kind of puppet, letting him pull the strings."

Lila shook her head sympathetically, but she had to summon every last ounce of reserve she had to keep from jumping up and doing cartwheels. She'd known it all along. Jack was somebody. And, of course, from as wealthy a family as her own. A matchless match, as far as she was concerned.

Yet she did as the occasion demanded and put on a solemn face. "That must have been really hard on you, Jack," she commiserated. "Just who is your father, anyway, that he's so used to controlling people?" Lila busily conjured up images of famous politicians, Hollywood movie moguls, and corporate magnates.

"Look, Lila, it's not important to know my

father's name or what he does. I'm trying to get away from all that. I want to be my own person, not just my father's son."

Lila was impressed. "I think I understand," she told him. "Sometimes I feel as if I'm nothing more than George Fowler's daughter." That was true, although more often than not, Lila herself was the first to let people know that she was the daughter of one of the richest men in Sweet Valley.

"I'm glad you understand." Jack reached over and squeezed Lila's hand gratefully. "I don't want to go back home until I've made it on my own—from the bottom up. I don't want any special favors from anyone just because I was born with a silver spoon in my mouth." Jack paused, tilting his head back and looking up at the purple sky.

"But sometimes"—he gave a forlorn sigh—"sometimes I miss my kid sister so much. That's the toughest part about being away from home. And this whole thing is so hard on her. Mom died a few years ago, so now it's just Valerie and Dad. That's her name—Valerie."

Lila heard such tenderness in his voice as he spoke about his little sister, she could barely resist melting into Jack's arms right then and there. *What a wonderful human being*, she thought. She sensed him relaxing as he continued to talk about Valerie.

"We used to have so much fun together,

21

exploring the woods in back of Grandpapa's cha-
let in Switzerland or hiding from Veronique. She
was our governess, this old Parisian woman. Of
course, Father made sure we were brought up
fluent in French, and he had us studying Latin,
as well, by the time I was ten and Valerie was
eight.''

Lila relaxed in her chair, incredibly happy to
have Jack opening up to her. But suddenly, his
reminiscences were cut short by the sound of a
car coming up the private road to Fowler Crest.
"Oh, no," she wailed. "Daddy's back. He must
have managed to find a flight home tonight after
all." Suddenly Lila was in a panic. Jack's quest
for independence was fine with her—in fact, she
was thoroughly impressed by him—but a rebellious son might not sit any better with her father
than a construction worker would.

Jack seemed to sense her predicament.
"Should I leave before your father sees me?" he
offered.

Lila nodded. "He—uh—doesn't allow me to
have boys over when no one else is here," she
lied. Actually when Mr. Fowler was away, Lila
pretty much did as she pleased. But she couldn't
tell Jack the truth, or he might think she was
ashamed of him. Which was hardly the case. In
fact, Lila felt more in love with him with each
passing minute.

But now the headlights of Mr. Fowler's limousine caught the front of the mansion as the car pulled up by the entranceway.

"Look, I parked at the bottom of the hill," Jack said. "I didn't think my old car would make it up here. So I can sneak out without being seen."

"I guess you ought to," Lila said, resigned. *But why now, when we were just getting to know each other!* she thought. She almost couldn't decide which was worse, risking her father's anger or letting Jack disappear just when he was beginning to talk about himself.

"Lila, one furious father is enough for me." Jack slipped into his Top-Siders and stuffed his towel and damp swimsuit into his knapsack. "But we'll see each other again. I can't go out much during the week because I have to be at work so early, but how about next weekend? Say Friday night?"

"I'd love to." Lila's smile was as genuine as the diamond pendant hanging around her neck.

"Great. I'll call you before then, OK?" Jack gave Lila a quick kiss on the cheek and vanished down the driveway, leaving her alone in the balmy night air.

An hour or so later, Lila sat on her canopied bed in her plush bedroom, cradling her pale-blue princess phone. She lifted the receiver and began putting it to her ear, then stayed her hand in midair. Finally, she slammed the receiver back down. She had promised Jack she would keep

23

his secret, and she intended to do so. She put the phone on the antique night table next to the bed and lay back on the pile of goose-down pillows. In her mind, she went over every word she and Jack had said to each other and pictured every line, every contour of his face. She touched the spot on her cheek where he had kissed her goodbye. He was so wonderful, so perfect. If only she could talk to someone about him! She thought she might burst if she had to hold in her good news any longer.

She reached over and touched the telephone again. What would it hurt if she made one little phone call, told just one person about Jack, and made sure the word didn't go any further? Her feelings for him were so special, she *had* to share them with someone. Jack would understand. He was that kind of guy.

Lila lifted the telephone receiver once again and quickly dialed Cara Walker's number. "Cara?" she said, when her friend answered the phone. "I've got to tell you the absolute best news. But you have to swear not to repeat a word of it. Swear? Cross your heart and hope to die?" And then Lila proceeded to tell Cara everything she knew about the most fabulous guy in Sweet Valley.

Three

"Look at all this paper." Elizabeth moaned. It was lunchtime, and she was sitting in the *Oracle* office behind a long table that was covered with heaps of newspaper clippings, typed pages, and handwritten notes, none of which seemed to be arranged in any order at all.

"Penny left you with a big job, eh?" Mr. Collins, Sweet Valley High English teacher and faculty adviser for the student paper, smiled at Elizabeth and put a comforting hand on her shoulder.

Penny Ayala, the editor of *The Oracle*, had come down with mononucleosis the previous week, and Elizabeth had volunteered to help put the next few issues of the newspaper together. It was a tough job, but working with Mr. Collins made it a lot more pleasant.

Young, handsome Roger Collins was more than just a popular teacher at Sweet Valley High. To many students he was also a friend. They could go to him if their grades were slipping or they were having trouble at home, and he would understand and help them to think their problems through. And with his athletic build, his strawberry-blond hair, and friendly blue eyes, he was also the focus of more schoolgirl crushes than any other teacher at Sweet Valley High. But right now, Elizabeth wasn't sure even Mr. Collins could help her sort out this mess.

"Liz, take it one step at a time. That's all you can do. First divide it all into past issues, the upcoming issue, and future issues. Then go through the material for the upcoming issue and call Penny about anything you don't know how to handle."

Elizabeth nodded. "You're right, Mr. Collins, and the sooner I get started, the better." She immediately began sifting through everything on Penny's desk. Around her, typewriters clacked, and the *Oracle* staff worked furiously to meet the deadline for the next issue.

As Mr. Collins left Elizabeth's side, she finished sorting the first pile of paper, then turned her attention to the next. On top of this pile was a black-and-white photograph. Elizabeth picked it up for a closer look and began giggling uncontrollably. It was a picture of Tad Johnson, a 240-pound linebacker for the Sweet Valley High football team, kissing a tiny teddy bear! In the background Elizabeth could just make out Jessica and the other cheerleaders, warming up before a game.

"John," she shouted, still chuckling, "did you take this picture?"

"What picture?" John Pfeifer, *The Oracle*'s sports editor, went over to where Elizabeth was standing. An amateur shutterbug, John sometimes helped Allen Walters, the paper's photographer. Now, looking at the photo Elizabeth had placed back down on the desk, he broke into a huge grin. "I wish I *had* taken this picture." He tapped the photo with the eraser end of his pencil. "It's a classic. But it's not mine."

"Where do you think it came from?" Elizabeth turned the photograph over for some clue, but the back was blank.

"Can't say," John answered. "I know Allen didn't take it. Yet another mystery of the day."

"Another?" asked Elizabeth.

"Sure. The first mystery's about that guy Jack who was at Lila's party. Everybody's trying to figure out where he came from. In fact, I just heard he was some kind of prince in disguise."

Elizabeth rolled her eyes. "Oh, now he's a prince? This rumor is really getting out of hand."

"Who's surprised?" John shrugged. "We both know Sweet Valley High has a hotter gossip circuit than Hollywood."

Elizabeth agreed. Cara had called Jessica with the news the night before, and Jessica had instantly related it to her twin. By this morning, the word was all over school: Jack was somebody, with a capital *S*. But exactly *who* was as mystifying as who had taken the picture on Elizabeth's desk.

"I think we should print it," Elizabeth announced.

"What, the rumor about Jack?" John asked with surprise.

"No, silly, the photo. I'm going to call Penny right now and get her OK."

Penny's mother answered the phone on the third ring. "Hi, Mrs. Ayala," Elizabeth said. "This is Liz Wakefield. Is Penny able to come to the phone?"

"Oh, hello, Liz, dear. Yes, Penny just woke up from a nap, and I think she'll be delighted to hear from you. Hold on, and I'll bring the phone into her room."

Penny sounded weak, but glad for some news from the outside world. Elizabeth told her about everything that was going on at school, including the rumor about Lila's prince, and then described the photograph she'd found.

"Oh, that sounds hysterical, Liz. Definitely use the picture," Penny said, laughing.

"But you don't know anything more about it than I do?" Elizabeth questioned.

"Not if Allen didn't take it."

The two girls speculated on who the photographer could be, but came up with nothing. After a few minutes' more discussion of *Oracle* business, they said goodbye.

Elizabeth replaced the telephone receiver.

"John," she called to the sports editor, who had returned to his desk at the back of the room, "Penny didn't know a thing about the picture."

John twisted his face into an expression of mock horror and hummed the theme from "The Twilight Zone."

Elizabeth giggled. "A photo from the fourth dimension. Is that what you think?"

"Anything's possible." John grinned.

"Maybe, but I'll bet there's a very down-to-earth solution to this puzzle," Elizabeth said as she rolled a clean sheet of paper into her typewriter. *A kiss for good luck before the big game*, she typed. *The secret of Tad Johnson's success on the football field is out of the bag. But still unknown is the identity of the photographer who took this picture. Will the phantom photographer please stand up?* She pulled the sheet out of the typewriter and clipped the photo of Tad to it. This was one mystery that wasn't going to go unsolved.

Jessica took a bowl of soggy-looking fruit salad from the cafeteria counter. "Yuck," she said to Cara Walker.

"Well, you can always bring your own food, like Lila did today." Cara gestured with her chin to where Lila sat, unwrapping her lunch.

"Poor thing," Jessica said sarcastically. "It's probably a butter and caviar sandwich."

"If you've got it, flaunt it," Cara said, helping herself to a plate of macaroni and cheese.

"Well, she does flaunt it," Jessica muttered. "Just like she was flaunting Jack all yesterday afternoon. I mean, she was showing him off like he was some kind of prize peacock or something."

"Yeah, I know," Cara affirmed. "But she doesn't look too happy with herself right now." Lila was sitting alone, a drawn expression on her face, barely picking at her lunch. "Should we go find out what's wrong?"

"Absolutely," Jessica replied, putting a dessert on her tray. Maybe, just maybe, Lila was upset because Jack had called her later and canceled the date she'd told Cara all about. Maybe he'd even told her he was interested in someone else—someone with blond hair and blue-green eyes, and the initials J.W., perhaps.

"Well, well," Lila exclaimed icily as Cara and Jessica sat down at the table. "If it isn't Benedict Arnold Wakefield, and her sidekick, Cara the Mouth."

Jessica gave Cara a sidelong glance and rolled her eyes. Then she turned toward Lila. "I can't imagine what you're talking about," she uttered in a voice that could have melted a glacier.

But Lila wasn't buying Jessica's act. "You know perfectly well what I mean, you traitor—throwing yourself all over *my* guy."

Oh, so now he's your guy, Jessica thought. But she said nothing.

"And you, Cara—I told you about Jack in confidence, and now it's all over school," Lila snapped. "I'd be better off making friends with a school of killer whales than with you two."

Jessica put her lunch tray down across the table from Lila, and Cara settled beside her. "Oh, come on, Lila. I was only trying to be nice to your guest of honor, and Cara was so excited by what you told her, she just *had* to share it with someone. You should understand that. You felt the same way, didn't you?" Jessica crafted the excuses like a seasoned pro—but to no avail.

"Well, thanks for nothing, guys," Lila muttered, pushing aside a cupful of shrimp salad.

"Hey, if you don't want that, I'll take it," Cara piped up. "The sandwich, too. This macaroni is probably hazardous to my health."

"Cara, give me one good reason why I should do you any favors," Lila snapped.

"Because I'm your friend. You know I am. Look, Lila, we didn't mean to upset you. Honest." Cara reached over and put a hand on Lila's shoulder in a conciliatory gesture. Lila shrugged it off, but a few seconds later, she pushed her lunch toward Cara. "I don't want it anyway," she mumbled.

"Ah, the proverbial olive branch—a sign of peace!" Jessica declared, reaching over and helping herself to a bit of shrimp.

"It's for her, not for you," Lila growled.

"OK, OK!" Jessica exclaimed. "Although I don't know why you're such a grouch today. Jack *is* taking you out, isn't he?" Jessica held her

31

breath and waited for a negative response, but instead Lila nodded. "You, not me, right?" Jessica continued, hoping there was some mistake.

"I suppose so," Lila submitted weakly.

Jessica felt her cheeks flush with anger and disappointment. So Jack was going out with Lila. It wasn't at all what Jessica wanted to hear. Still that didn't mean the battle was over. Jessica had every intention of getting Jack interested in her. It would simply take a little more planning. But right then, she wondered what Lila could possibly be so upset about. If Jack had asked *her* for a date, she wouldn't be sitting around moping.

"So what's the problem, Lila? If Jack's taking you out, why don't you look happier?" Jessica speared another piece of shrimp with her fork, and this time Lila didn't protest. Instead she put her head in her hands, her wavy, light-brown hair falling across her face.

"Yeah, Fowler, spill it," Cara demanded. "What's the sad story?"

Lila lifted her head up and peered at Cara. "Do you really care?"

"Yes!" Cara and Jessica chorused in unison, ready to devour this newest bit of information.

"It's my father," Lila told them. "He's absolutely furious with me."

"Why?" Cara asked, starting in on Lila's sandwich—it *was* butter and caviar after all.

"Well, somehow this expensive vase got broken at the party." Lila moaned. "And then the drain to the pool got all clogged up. And the worst thing is that all Dad's gold cuff links and tie clips have disappeared."

"Really?" Jessica asked, her blue-green eyes wide with surprise. "Who do you think would have taken them?"

Lila shrugged. "Beats me. I think maybe they just got misplaced. You know, the maid moved them or something."

"Yeah, I remember Bruce once telling me that Mrs. Patman's emerald-and-platinum choker vanished one day," Jessica said, looking across the cafeteria to where rich, handsome Bruce Patman was talking to some of his friends from the tennis team. "It turned up later in a drawer where they kept stuff for their dog. It seemed one of the servants thought it was a dog collar."

Lila and Cara giggled. "Hey, speaking of Bruce," Cara said to Lila, "where was he yesterday, anyway? I didn't see him at your party."

"That's because I didn't invite him," Lila answered. "You wouldn't believe what his father said about mine at the last town meeting."

"Spare us," Jessica uttered. "I'm sure we've heard it all before."

Two of the wealthiest men in Southern California, George Fowler and Henry Wilson Patman were rivals in business and in everything else, too. Mr. Fowler was constantly working to modernize, computerize, and automate every bit of Sweet Valley, while Mr. Patman was fighting to keep every stone exactly the way it had been when his grandfather sat on the town board. The Patman-Fowler feud had been going on for as long as Jessica could remember. She found the whole thing absurd, not to mention tedious.

"Besides," Lila continued, darting an icy glance in Bruce's direction, "he told me he had better things to do than to go to some juvenile pool party. He said he had very important work to finish for the Sweet Valley Centennial Committee."

Bruce had just been elected president of the committee in a triumphant win over Ken Matthews, though his victory had been marred by Regina Morrow's departure for the clinic in Switzerland. Much to everyone's surprise, especially Jessica's, Bruce had fallen hard and fast for Regina and for once had thought about somebody besides himself. But with Regina gone, Bruce was his usual egotistical self and was wasting no opportunity to brag about his position as the centennial student committee president.

"Oh, big man," Jessica declared sarcastically. "It's just as well." Bruce was no great favorite of Jessica's either, ever since their brief though much-talked-about romance had ended disastrously.

"But why waste any more breath on Bruce," Lila said. "Right now I have to figure out what

34

I'm going to do about my father!" She slapped the edge of the cafeteria table in frustration.

"I don't know what you're worrying about," Cara said. "Your father can replace all those things. Well, maybe not the vase, but he can get one just as good. I mean it's not like he can't afford it or anything."

"No, you've missed the whole point," Lila wailed. "It's not about the cuff links. It's about my seeing Jack."

"What's that got to do with it?" Jessica said sharply, reminded once again of Lila's date with the mysterious, handsome boy.

"Well, it would have been hard enough to tell my dad about him before, but now that he's so mad about the pool and everything, it'll really be impossible. Until Jack sets things straight with his family—whoever they are—he'll never pass the test with my father. I don't dare say a word to him." The corners of Lila's mouth turned down.

"That's tough," Cara said sympathetically. "But you're not going to let that keep you from seeing Jack, are you?"

"No way," Lila asserted defiantly. "I'll just have to meet him on the sly. Not that it'll be so hard." A bitter note crept into her voice. "Dad's hardly around anyway." It was well known to both Cara and Jessica that Mr. Fowler's long and frequent business trips angered Lila. "Anyway," Lila continued, "even if he were around, nothing can stand in the way of true love!"

Jessica took the last bite of Lila's shrimp salad and swallowed hard. *That's what you think*, she thought, glancing at Lila. *But we'll see about that!*

Jessica lounged beside the Wakefields' pool, an open copy of Strindberg's *Miss Julie* next to her. She had balked at first when they'd been assigned the play in English class, but to her surprise it was turning out to be pretty good. Miss Julie was a fascinating character as far as Jessica was concerned. Rotten, but fascinating.

Now, however, Jessica couldn't concentrate on a word of her reading. In her mind, she kept seeing Jack's suntanned face and the special smile he'd managed to sneak her as she'd been leaving the party. Didn't that smile mean anything? Why had he made a date with Lila instead of her? Jessica racked her brain for a reason. What did Lila have that she didn't? She made a mental list: One—loads of money; two—tons of money; three—piles and piles of money. Elizabeth was always telling her that money wasn't the most important thing in the world, but Jessica wasn't so sure. It could certainly make life easier. But was that why Jack had asked Lila out? It didn't make sense. Jack had run away from his father and his own family fortune to make it on his own. There had to be another reason.

From inside the house came the faint ringing of the telephone. Jessica sat straight up and held her breath. Maybe this was the call she'd been waiting for. The ringing stopped, and a few seconds later, Alice Wakefield, the twins' mother, poked her head out of the sliding glass doors that led to the patio and the pool.

"Jess," Mrs. Wakefield shouted, "it's for you."

Jessica raced inside to her father's study, then composed herself before she picked up the phone. "Hello?" she said serenely.

"Hi, Jessica," came a male voice. "This is Jack."

A slow smile spread across Jessica's face. "Jack! What a nice surprise. How are you?"

"Good, and you?"

"Just fine," Jessica replied. "What's up?"

"I was wondering if you'd like to go out sometime this week," Jack proposed.

"That sounds nice," Jessica said nonchalantly, playing it as cool as only she could. "When did you have in mind?"

"How does the day after tomorrow sound?"

Wednesday, Jessica thought. That was two days before Lila would even have a chance at him. "Wednesday's perfect."

"How about if I pick you up at your house at eight, and we can figure out what we feel like doing then?"

"Great," Jessica replied. She made conversation with him for a few minutes and then gave him her address.

37

"So, I'll see you on Wednesday," Jack said. "I'm looking forward to it."

"Me, too," replied Jessica.

"Bye, Jess. Take care."

"I will, Jack. See you." Jessica put down the receiver and gave a shriek of excitement.

"Jess, what are you yelling about?" Mrs. Wakefield called from the other room.

"Oh, nothing, Mom," she called back. *Nothing except about the most gorgeous, charming, mysteriously exciting guy in the whole world,* she added to herself. Let Lila sneak behind her father's back. Jessica was convinced that she wouldn't be doing it for long. Because soon Jack would be eating out of Jessica's hand, and Lila would be nothing more than a name in his past.

Four

"How does this look?" Jessica stood in the middle of Elizabeth's cream-colored bedroom and modeled a slinky, royal-blue dress. It fell softly to just below her knees, with a slit up both sides to midthigh. "Casual but elegant, right?"

"Right," Elizabeth answered as she looked up from an article for the next issue of *The Oracle*. "But I just bought that dress last week, and I've only worn it once."

"Sexy, too," Jessica added, ignoring her sister's comment.

Elizabeth put her work down on the table she used as a desk and stuck her pencil behind one ear. "Yes, Jess, it looks absolutely terrific, but who said you could wear it?"

Jessica inspected herself in Elizabeth's full-length mirror. "Well, you're not going out tonight. That means you're not going to wear it," Jessica observed. "So I figured—"

"Exactly what you always figure—that you can come in here and take anything you want."

"Hey, what's bothering you tonight, Liz?" Jessica glanced at her sister with annoyance. "You're usually so generous with your clothes. If I'd known you were going to throw a hundred and thirty-seven fits, I wouldn't have put the dress on in the first place. Jeez, ever since you got forced into doing all that extra work on *The Oracle*, you've just been one laugh after another."

Elizabeth watched her twin begin to take the dress off. "For your information, I didn't get forced into anything. I wanted to help Penny. It's a chance to learn a lot about how the paper's put together. But maybe all the extra hours *are* making me a little tense." Elizabeth's voice softened. "And I'm sorry if I snapped at you. It's just that the last time I lent you something to wear, I found it days later, crumpled into a little ball under your bed."

Jessica let the dress slip back over her head. "I promise to take care of this, Liz. After my date, I'll hang it right back up in your closet. Really, I will."

"And if you don't, you agree to do all my house chores for a week?"

Jessica thought for a moment. "Well, I wouldn't go that far."

"Jess . . ."

"Look, I absolutely, positively give you my word that I'll return the dress exactly the way I found it."

"Well, OK." Elizabeth finally gave in. "Although I must say, I wish you were going to be putting it to better use."

"Ah-ha!" Jessica cried, spinning around to face her twin. "*That's* the real reason why you're so crabby tonight. You're upset that I'm going out with Jack."

Elizabeth shrugged.

"What have you got against him, Liz? You met him yourself, and you have to admit that he's pretty special. Listen, he's handsome, right?"

Elizabeth nodded.

"And he's polite."

"I suppose so."

"And charming. And fun. Liz, all the other kids thought he was great."

"I know, Jess, and he probably is, but—"

"But what?" Jessica demanded in exasperation. She sank down next to her sister on the bed. "You're the one who's always telling me to give people a chance. You're the one who thinks the very best about everyone. Why not Jack? It's really not like you at all."

"I know," Elizabeth agreed. "But I just have this funny feeling about him. I mean, I know he acts really considerate and all that, but what kind of guy would date two girls at the same time?" Elizabeth nervously fingered the hem of her yellow sun dress, avoiding her twin's frosty stare. She knew she was making Jessica feel hurt and angry, and she felt terrible about it, but there

41

was something about Jack that didn't seem right to her. She just couldn't put her finger on what it was.

"Don't you see?" Jessica asked impatiently. "That's exactly why he *is* taking Lila out. I mean, he was practically a perfect stranger, and she invited him to her party, then introduced him to everyone. He owes it to her to go out with her once."

Elizabeth looked at her sister doubtfully.

"Liz, don't stare at me like that. It'll be OK. I'm sure I'm the one he really likes."

Elizabeth got up and stretched. "I hope that's true. I don't want to see you get hurt, Jess, and this is a guy you don't know the first thing about."

Jessica's eyes narrowed dangerously, and, like a tea kettle reaching the boiling point, she uttered a piercing squeal. "How could any sister of mine be so dull, dull, dull? The mystery around Jack is part of what makes him so exciting!"

Elizabeth made one last stab at reasoning with her sister. "But why is he so secretive? What's he hiding?"

Jessica stood up, walked over to Elizabeth, and grabbed her by the arm. "Look, maybe you're the kind of person who has to know exactly what she's getting and get exactly what she knows— safe, reliable, never anything left to chance. But I like a little intrigue in my life. It keeps things interesting. So you, Miss Stick-in-the-Mud Worrywart, can just keep your worries to yourself where I'm concerned." Jessica spun on her heels and left the room, through the bathroom that connected her room to her sister's.

Elizabeth sighed. She hadn't meant to act like a mother hen, but she had a funny feeling about Jack. She was afraid that once again, Jessica was headed for trouble.

At precisely eight o'clock, the doorbell chimed. Jessica rushed to answer it, a radiant smile on her lips. Her smile brightened even more when she saw Jack. Dressed in camel-colored slacks, a button-down shirt in light-blue Egyptian cotton, brown loafers, and a matching belt, he looked as if he'd just stepped out of the pages of *Gentleman's Quarterly*. He grinned down at her, his green-flecked eyes drinking in her appearance.

"You look lovely, Jessica," he said, bringing his left arm around from behind his back and producing a single, long-stemmed red rose.

"Oh, Jack. How perfect." Jessica took the flower and held it to her nose, inhaling deeply. "It's beautiful."

Jack waited politely on the doorstep, watching her. "Oh, gosh, I'm sorry to keep you standing there," Jessica said suddenly. "Why don't you come in? I'm sure Mom and Dad would like to meet you." She took Jack's arm with one hand, holding the rose in the other, and ushered him into the living room. "Mom, Dad, this is Jack," she said proudly.

Tall, dark-haired Ned Wakefield got up from the living-room sofa and extended his hand. If he'd noticed that Jessica had introduced Jack by only his first name, he said nothing about it. "Good to meet you," he remarked heartily.

"Nice to meet you, too, Mr. Wakefield. And you, Mrs. Wakefield." Jack shook their hands in turn.

"Oh, did you bring Jessica a rose?" Alice Wakefield asked, spotting the flower in her daughter's hand. "How lovely."

Jack smiled. "I got it at the new florist shop in the mall. Have you been over there yet? The owner does the most beautiful Japanese arrangements."

Jessica listened as Jack made conversation with her parents. They seemed utterly charmed by him. And as far as she was concerned, they had every reason to be. What did Elizabeth know, anyway? Jessica tilted her face upward and sent a tiny, almost imperceptible scowl in the direction of her twin's upstairs bedroom. Then she turned her attention back to Jack and gave him an adoring look.

He responded by moving toward her and putting his arm around her shoulder. Jessica felt a bolt of electricity shoot through her at his touch.

"Ready to go?" he asked.

"Absolutely," Jessica agreed, impatient for a chance to be alone with him.

Goodbyes were said, and finally they were closing the door behind them. At last Jessica had Jack all to herself.

Her pulse racing with excitement, Jessica breathed in the evening air.

"Great night for taking a walk on the beach," Jack said, his arm still around Jessica's shoulder. "Wouldn't you say?"

"My thoughts exactly," Jessica answered, snuggling closer to him. This promised to be just the night she'd been dreaming of.

Jack led her toward a rusty old Rambler, parked in front of the Wakefields' house, and unlocked the passenger door. "I wish I could offer you a ride with more style," he apologized, "but when I left home, my days of fancy cars ended." He pulled open the door and held it for her.

Jessica climbed into the car as though it were a Rolls-Royce. She'd often told Elizabeth that she rode in only the best cars and that she wouldn't be caught dead in something like the second-hand Datsun Todd drove. But suddenly, Jack's old Rambler seemed like the classiest car in all of California. "I like your car," she informed him as they headed down Calico Drive and then out toward the beach. "If it's good enough for you, it's good enough for me."

"Thanks, Jess." The breeze from Jack's

window rippled through his thick, honey-colored hair. "I earned every penny for it myself," he said. Jessica noted the dignity that surrounded his words. "There's nothing like being able to make your own way," he added.

"Yeah, that's the thing about still being in school," Jessica remarked. "I really have to depend on my parents for everything. Of course, I do take baby-sitting jobs whenever I can, and I've had a couple of after-school jobs, too," she added quickly. She didn't mention that her after-school work experience was limited to a brief stint as a clerical assistant in her father's law office. That job had lasted a grand total of two weeks, and then only because she had her eye on the cute guy in the offices across the hall. But this was no time for true confessions. From everything Jack had said so far, independence was at the very top of his "must have" list. And Jessica intended to make it very clear that she had it.

As the car sped along, the stores and restaurants gave way to low, rolling sand dunes, the lights from an occasional beach house spilling out onto the road. In the distance, Jessica could hear the ocean waves crashing against the shore, and a tangy smell of salt and sea filled her nostrils.

At the end of the road, Jack turned the car into a small, deserted beachfront parking lot. He shut off the motor and let himself out of the car, once again coming around to Jessica's side to open her door.

"Madam?" he joked, offering his arm.

Jessica took it, gazing up at his handsome face, and they began to walk toward the beach. She stopped looking at him only long enough to bend down and slip off her sandals, wriggling her toes in the cool, moist sand as she stood up again.

"Good idea," Jack said, quickly following Jessica's example. He left his loafers and socks on the edge of the blacktop and joined her on the sand.

The ocean wind blew softly as they strolled down to the water's edge. "It's so vast, so wild," Jack reflected as he stared out at the seemingly boundless sea. "It makes you feel like nothing more than one of these tiny grains of sand. Know what I mean?"

"Mmm." Jessica nodded. "But at the same time, there's something about it that makes you feel so alive." She stuck her foot out so that the icy water lapped at her toes. "Brrr. Cold," she declared, snuggling closer to Jack.

Jack wrapped both his arms around her, and she rested her head against his broad chest. They were silent for some time, just feeling each other's nearness and contemplating the great, dark ocean. "I can't imagine ever living too far away from the sea," Jack said finally.

"Me neither," agreed Jessica, slowly rubbing

her palm up and down Jack's back. "But does that mean you grew up on the West Coast?" she asked curiously.

Jack hedged. "Well, not exactly."

"Oh, the East Coast, then."

"Look, I'd really rather not talk about it," Jack declared, a touch snappishly. Jessica felt him tense up, and he loosened his hold on her.

"OK, I'm sorry," Jessica said, the hurt in her voice as clear as a bright summer's day.

"Oh, Jess." Jack was instantly contrite. "No, *I'm* the one who's sorry. Please understand; I didn't mean to snap at you. It's just that I'm trying so hard to leave my old life behind. I guess I just don't like to talk about it much."

That's the understatement of the year, Jessica thought. But as Jack gently drew her into his arms once more, all was instantly forgiven.

"Besides," Jack whispered in her ear, "it's so much more interesting to talk about you. There are so many things I'd like to find out."

"There are?" Jessica felt a surge of elation course through her body.

"Sure. Like for starters, I want to hear about what it's like growing up as a twin."

Jessica laughed. "Yeah, a lot of people wonder about that. Most of the time it's great. Liz is the best sister in the whole world. And it comes in pretty handy now and then to have someone who looks exactly like you!"

She told Jack about the time she'd gotten in

over her head with a fast college crowd and a guy named Scott, and had ended up stranded with him overnight in a cabin in the woods. She hadn't been able to make it back in time for school the next morning, and Elizabeth had not only covered for her to their parents, but she'd also taken an exam twice—once for herself, and once pretending to be Jessica!

"Boy, was Liz mad at me when I got back!" Jessica exclaimed.

The conversation moved from Jessica's family to her friends and her courses at school. Jack wanted to hear about it all. Not that Jessica minded, but even she eventually felt that she had talked about herself enough for one night. "And thus endeth the tales of Jessica Wakefield!" she concluded, slipping her arms around Jack's waist. She could feel his muscles rippling under the thin cotton of his shirt.

"You're a great storyteller, Jess," Jack said huskily. "I think I'll name a star after you." He and Jessica looked upward. Every star in the sky sparkled like a cut diamond. "That one," Jack proclaimed, reaching his finger out to point toward the star. "Because it shines more brightly than all the rest."

Jessica followed his outstretched arm with her eyes. "But, Jack, that's the North Star!"

"Not to me, it's not. Not any longer." Jack caressed Jessica's cheek with his fingertips. "From now on that star is called Jessica, and every time I look at it, I'll think about you and this wonderful evening.''

Jessica's heart did flip-flops, and her pulse raced. This had to be true love! She lifted her face up toward his, her gaze tracing his eyes, his straight nose, chiseled cheekbones, his strong jaw, and full mouth.

Slowly, gently, he lowered his lips onto hers and took her in a long, lingering embrace.

Five

Elizabeth kicked absentmindedly at a pebble as she walked to Penny Ayala's house the following afternoon. Her arms were loaded with folders for the next issue of *The Oracle*. Now that Penny's illness was no longer contagious, Elizabeth wanted to go over all the work she'd done thus far.

One of the folders held all the photos Elizabeth planned to print, including the picture of Tad Johnson, and also two more phantom photos that had been shoved under the door of the *Oracle* office. She had found them that morning. The first was a snapshot of Sweet Valley High's principal, Mr. Cooper, crouched under a desk in a very undignified position, hunting for something. She could tell who it was because the top of his bald head—it had earned him the nickname "Chrome Dome" among the students—was shining underneath the desk. The second picture showed Bob Russo—the strictest, toughest teacher in the school—on the campus

51

lawn, petting a tiny, adorable kitten, an expression of pure delight on his usually stern face.

Elizabeth mused over the pictures as she turned into the walkway that led up to the Ayalas' two-story white house. She had no idea who the photographer was, but she wished fervently that she could find out. Whoever it was showed talent, and *The Oracle* could definitely use another good staff photographer.

"Hello?" Elizabeth called through the screen door, knocking on the door frame.

"Hi," said a brunette, opening the screen door wide. "Come on in," she invited in a friendly voice. "I'm Penny's sister, Tina."

Elizabeth recognized the girl from school—one of the younger kids, a ninth-grader, Elizabeth believed. "And I'm Liz Wakefield."

"I know." Tina grinned. "Everyone at Sweet Valley High has heard of you and Jessica."

Elizabeth blushed modestly. "I've seen you around, also," she returned, "but I never realized you were Penny's sister. You don't look anything alike." Penny was tall and lanky and fair-haired, but Tina was small, dark, and plump, with a spray of freckles across the bridge of her nose.

"Yeah, sometimes even *I* find it hard to believe we're sisters!"

As they talked, Tina led Elizabeth up the stairs to a bedroom door plastered with the front pages of newspapers from all over the world. Elizabeth knew Penny's dream was to become the editor of an international newspaper. She wanted it as much as Elizabeth wanted someday to be a well-known author. Penny was one of the very few people with whom Elizabeth had shared her secret ambition, because Penny had her sights set in a similar manner.

Tina Ayala pushed open the door to her sister's room. "Pen?" she called. "Liz Wakefield's here to see you."

Elizabeth took a step inside the room. Like Penny's desk at the *Oracle* office, every surface was covered with note pads, papers, pencils, and pens. One whole wall was covered with shelves holding books and encyclopedias.

At the far corner of the room, Penny was sitting up in bed, two pillows propped behind her head. She was very pale, and there were dark circles under her eyes, but she smiled brightly at her visitor. "Liz, it's so good to see you. Here, pull up a chair." She motioned to an armchair not far from the side of the bed.

"I'll leave you two alone," Tina excused herself as Elizabeth walked over to Penny. "Bye, Liz."

"See you in school, Tina," Elizabeth replied over her shoulder. She put her files and folders on the rust-colored shag carpeting and sank into the chair. "How are you feeling, Penny?" she asked.

Penny made a face. "I'll feel better when I can

stay awake for more than half an hour at a time," she answered dryly. "Every time I try to read, I end up falling asleep. And I'm not doing much better with the TV, either." She nodded toward the television on a table by the foot of her bed. "But the doctor says I should be doing a lot better by next week. I might even be back at school by then."

Elizabeth shook her head sympathetically. "It's the hardest thing in the world to lie in bed and do absolutely nothing, isn't it?"

"You can say that again," Penny confirmed. "But now that you're here, I've got someone to help keep me occupied—and awake—for a while. So what did you bring me?"

"I'm afraid there's enough here to keep you busy until the middle of summer vacation," Elizabeth said. "Penny, I don't know how you manage to keep on top of things and put the paper out right on time every week."

"Oh, you get used to it," Penny said lightly, reaching for the material Elizabeth was handing her.

"That top folder has all the feature articles in it," Elizabeth explained, "including a story I asked Robin Wilson to do on the flying course she and some of the other kids from school are taking with students from Sweet Valley College."

Penny opened the folder excitedly, like a child opening presents on Christmas morning. "I didn't realize how much I missed working on the paper until just now," Penny reflected. "You know, every time a deadline comes up, I tear my hair out trying to meet it, and I ask myself whether I really want to go through this for the rest of my life, on one newspaper after another. But then, when I'm away from it for too long, I miss the energy of all those people working together to put out something they can be proud of."

Eagerly Penny picked up Robin's article and began to read. "Hey, this is really good!" she observed. "I didn't know Robin could write like this."

"She used to write all the time," Elizabeth explained, "before she lost all that weight. Remember? When she was the butt of everyone's jokes instead of the girl all the boys want to date?"

Penny nodded her head.

"She used to write because she needed some kind of outlet, a bit of comfort," Elizabeth continued. "Then when her life did that turnaround and she got onto the cheering squad and everything, she gave it up. I'm trying to encourage her to start again."

"She should," Penny agreed. "She's got a terrific style." She finished Robin's article and put it to one side of her, going on to the next few stories. But soon her eyelids began to droop.

"Penny, I think I'd better go soon and let you

sleep," Elizabeth said. "But before I leave, there's something I have to show you. Remember that picture of Tad Johnson I told you about over the phone?"

"Oh, yeah," Penny recalled, fighting to keep her eyes open. "Did you bring it with you? I'm dying to see it."

"That, and two more," Elizabeth told her, producing the photos.

The corners of Penny's mouth turned up as she looked at the first picture. At the other two, she broke into a huge grin, and finally a broad laugh. "Print them!" she ordered. "They're great!"

"Yes, ma'am!" Elizabeth declared.

"And one more thing," Penny said, trying to stifle a yawn. "You're the paper's best journalist, Liz, and every journalist is something of a detective. See if you can find out who's taking these pictures. I'd like to offer this photographer a position as a staff photographer."

"I hoped you'd say that," Elizabeth replied. "I'll do my best. And now, I think I'd better let you rest. I'll leave everything here. You can look it over, and I'll come get it tomorrow. You can tell me all your suggestions then. OK?"

"Oh, don't go," Penny protested sleepily, her voice growing weak. "I don't need to nap . . . just have to close my eyes for a second. . . ." She stretched back on her bed, and before she could finish her sentence, she was fast asleep.

"Sweet dreams," Elizabeth whispered. She let herself out of Penny's room and headed outside.

"Good practice," Jessica said as she and Cara headed toward the school parking lot and the Wakefields' red Fiat convertible, which Jessica and Elizabeth sometimes used. "That new cheer we're working on is hot!"

"Really," Cara confirmed. "But that split at the end of it is a killer."

"Cara," Jessica reprimanded her friend, "no one ever told you that being a cheerleader was all fun and games. You have to work at it to be the best. Look at Annie."

Cara pouted. "Oh, so now Annie Whitman's your best buddy? When did that happen?"

"Don't be silly." Jessica unlocked the door on the driver's side of the Fiat and opened it. She threw her books and cheering uniform in the back, then climbed in, reaching across to open the passenger's side. "*You're* my best buddy," she asserted when Cara was settled next to her. "It's just that Annie really knows how to work for what she wants. You have to respect her for it." Jessica started the car and exited the parking lot.

Cara eyed her friend suspiciously. "You know, Jess, that doesn't sound at all like something you'd say. As a matter of fact, I seem to remember your telling me not too long ago that it was too bad you couldn't have all the fun and attention of being a cheerleader without all the sweat. Now, all of a sudden, you can't stop blabbing about working for what you want."

Jessica blushed. In her mind, she could hear Jack's deep, rich voice talking about earning his own way and working for his independence. But she couldn't tell this to Cara. In fact she hadn't even mentioned the previous night's date to her friend. Despite the fact that not one second of the day had gone by when she hadn't thought of Jack, she didn't intend to tell anyone at school about him. Not until Lila was officially out of the picture.

"Well?" Cara's voice broke into Jessica's reverie. "What gives? What's this work business all about?" she demanded.

"I honestly don't know what you're talking about, Cara." Jessica made a left turn and headed toward the Dairi Burger, a fast-food place that was a hangout for many of the kids from Sweet Valley High. "I mean, I'm co-captain of the cheering team. It's my job to make sure that all the squad members work their hardest and perform their best. It's as simple as that." She flashed Cara a look that said "sincere," with a capital S.

"Well, OK, Jess. If you say so," Cara murmured, but she looked doubtful.

"I say so because that's the way it is," Jessica stated emphatically, pulling into the Dairi Burger parking lot. She turned off the ignition and quickly pulled a brush through her blond hair before getting out.

"Oh, listen," Cara informed her, as they entered the Dairi Burger, "I told Lila she could meet us here. I hope that's all right with you."

Jessica groaned inwardly. Of all the people she didn't want to see right now. . . . Lila would be sure to monopolize the conversation with talk of Jack, and Jessica didn't want to share even the *idea* of him with anyone else. Besides, Lila had been annoyed with her since the party, and she'd taken every opportunity to get in any cutting barbs she could manage.

Jessica had successfully avoided Lila all day at school, but now she could see her waving wildly from one of the booths at the back of the restaurant. It was too late for Jessica to back out and go home. She was already inside. She steeled herself.

"Cara, Jess. Over here," Lila called loudly. The girls made their way over to her. "I thought you'd never get here," Lila said as they slid into the booth. "Did you have to walk, poor dears?"

"No, practice just went late," Cara explained. "We came in the Wakefields' Fiat."

"Oh?" Lila focused her attention on Jessica. "Are they letting you drive again?" Jessica's parents had forbidden her to use the car several times over the past year, the result of everything from a badly dented front fender to several traffic tickets too many. "Well, I guess you'd better take

59

advantage of it while it lasts," Lila added bitingly.

"I guess so," Jessica said calmly, refusing to let Lila get to her.

"And why were you allowed to drive to school today, anyway?" Lila persisted. "I thought you were only allowed to use the car on special occasions."

Jessica grinned slyly. "I told my parents I had volunteered to drive over to the mall to pick up those new pompoms we ordered for the cheering squad."

"But I thought Sandy Bacon was doing that," Cara put in.

"That's true. But I *did* volunteer to do it," Jessica said smugly. "I just let Sandy volunteer harder."

Cara giggled. "Now *that's* the Jessica Wakefield I know and love."

Jessica grinned. "Well, as Lila said, I'd better take advantage of that car while I can. And now I think I'll go up and get some food. I'm absolutely famished after that practice."

"Oh, can you order for me, too?" Cara asked, sweeping her fingers through her long, dark hair.

"Why not?" Jessica offered. "I'll even order for you, Lila." She shot Lila one of her patented fake smiles. "What'll it be? Two clam specials?"

Lila and Cara groaned in unison. "Ugh. Don't even say that, Jess. Just thinking about those clam specials is dangerous," Cara said. "Get me a cheeseburger and a chocolate shake."

"I'll take a fish sandwich and a Tab," Lila put in, as Jessica left the table.

When she got back, Lila had already steered the conversation to the inevitable subject. A shrimp roll and a Coke later, Jessica was still trying every trick she knew to keep from paying attention to Lila's incessant chatter about Jack.

First she twisted around in her seat, staring at all the other people in the Dairi Burger and amusing herself by making up stories about each of them. For example, she decided that the nerdy little guy sitting in the corner by himself, poring over a dull-looking textbook, led a secret night life as a popular ladies' man. And that the man walking through the door with a cap pulled low over his face and a pair of dark glasses was a notorious bank robber.

But Jessica had the most fun imagining things about people she knew. She almost laughed out loud when her gaze came to rest on DeeDee Gordon and her boyfriend, Bill Chase, sharing an ice-cream sundae a few booths away. What if, she told herself, DeeDee suddenly developed a giant wart on the middle of her nose as she sat eating her ice cream? Jessica pictured Bill's face, and then DeeDee's, when she discovered what had happened to her. Jessica found this fantasy particularly satisfying because she'd never quite forgiven Bill and DeeDee for falling in love at a time when she herself was determined to keep Bill wrapped around her little finger.

But eventually Jessica had gone through everyone in the restaurant, and Lila was still holding forth on the wonders of Jack. "I just think the whole idea of a famous, important person disguised as a mere construction worker is incredibly romantic," she gushed.

One side of Jessica's upper lip curled in a disgusted sneer. That was *her* guy Lila was talking about, *her* Jack. Forget DeeDee Gordon with a wart. How would Lila look with one on her nose?

"I almost can't wait for tomorrow night," Lila was saying now. "I wish so badly that our date was tonight. But Jack has to get up at five-thirty every morning for work, so he doesn't go out much during the week."

Oh, not much at all, Jessica thought, remembering the feeling of his lips on hers.

"But it's just one day away," Lila continued, twisting a strand of hair around her index finger. "One more day, and he's all mine."

That's what you think, Jessica thought. Then she looked at Lila's face, so eager with anticipation, glowing at the thought of her handsome prince in disguise. And for the merest fraction of a second, Jessica almost felt sorry for her friend; Lila really was head over heels in love.

But so was Jessica! Her bud of sympathy died without flowering. She listened to the rest of

Lila's monologue without an ounce of pity. She remembered the old saying, "All's fair in love and war." Well, this was both. And judging from the previous night on the beach, Jessica felt sure that she was the one who would end up the winner.

As the girls finally prepared to leave the restaurant, Jessica allowed herself a private smile. By the time the weekend was over, Jack would be hers!

Six

On Monday morning, Lila nearly floated into school. She moved through the hallways with a faraway smile on her lips, oblivious to the noisy chatter of those around her. Every so often, she would laugh softly to herself, as if reliving some special moment that only she could see.

Jessica was at her locker, reaching up for her notebook, when she caught sight of Lila, that dreamy expression on her face. Jessica's hand froze in midair, and an icy numbness set in. That wasn't the look of someone who'd been jilted over the weekend, whose most cherished dream had been shattered. On the contrary, Lila showed every indication of having spent the past few days in paradise.

Jessica grabbed her notebook frantically, slammed her locker shut, and jammed the combination lock in place. As Lila drifted toward her, Jessica stepped directly in her path.

"Oh, Jessica," Lila said, snapping out of her

reverie. "How nice to see you. Did you have a good weekend?"

Now Jessica *knew* there was something wrong. Lila had acted snappishly toward her all the previous week, but suddenly that day she was Ms. Good Humor herself. "Nothing out of the ordinary," Jessica informed her.

"What?" Lila said, obviously back in her own little Never-Never Land.

"My weekend," Jessica stated flatly. "It was nothing special. You *did* ask how my weekend was."

"Yes," Lila murmured.

Jessica fidgeted with the gold lavaliere around her neck, a present from her parents on her sixteenth birthday. Finally she took a deep breath. "And how was your weekend?" she asked, almost afraid to hear the answer.

"Jessica, it was the absolute best weekend of my entire life!" Lila hugged her books to her chest and sighed contentedly.

"Why's that?" Jessica's fists were clenched at her side, her knuckles white.

"Jack." Lila uttered that one syllable as if it were the key to all the secrets of the universe.

"You mean things went well with him on Friday?" Jessica asked with stupefaction.

"On Friday," Lila echoed blissfully, "and Saturday, and yesterday, too."

Jessica couldn't believe what she was hearing.

65

There *had* to be some mistake. But another look at Lila's ecstatic face told her it was true.

"So—uh—when are you going to see him again?" Jessica asked, her words fighting through a sea of despair.

"Next Friday, of course. Because Jack can't go out on weekdays."

"Yes, I recall your mentioning that." A tiny glimmer of hope surfaced in the waters of Jessica's unhappiness. Jack had used that very excuse on Lila last week, to leave him free for her. Maybe Lila wasn't out of the picture yet, but Jessica had four long days to arrange things more to her liking!

The ringing bell signaled three more minutes until the beginning of the next period. Around Jessica and Lila, students stepped up their pace.

"I have to go," Lila said, coming back to reality for just a moment. "I've got a quiz next period, so I'd better not be late. See you, Jess."

"Right," Jessica responded curtly. She watched Lila float down the hall. *Well, let her be happy,* she thought. *This battle's not over yet!*

But by lunchtime, Jessica's spirits had taken another nose dive. The word of Lila's romance had blazed through the Sweet Valley High grapevine like wildfire, and all she'd heard throughout the morning was Jack and Lila, Lila and Jack. Even to Jessica, the pairing of their names was beginning to have a certain natural ring, like Romeo and Juliet, or Antony and Cleopatra. True, she'd heard that Lila had learned nothing more about Jack's real identity, but it was hard to deny that after this weekend they were very much a couple.

At first Jessica had directed all her anger toward Lila, plotting ways to sabotage her blossoming romance. But eventually, she'd had to admit that she couldn't blame Lila for going after what she wanted. Anyone else would have done the same thing. In fact, Jessica *was* doing it. But perhaps she wasn't going about it in the right way. Maybe another approach would go over better with Jack. But what? Her methods seemed to have worked just fine on numerous other guys. No, Jessica concluded, it wasn't Lila's fault, and it wasn't her own.

Finally, she had to face the facts: The trouble lay with Jack. Jack, who had held her and whispered tender words to her. Jack, who would always think of Jessica when he looked at the North Star. Jack, the prince of romance. Jessica's mind whirled with rage. How could he do this to her? What kind of guy was he, anyway? Maybe she should have listened to her sister. Maybe Elizabeth had been right.

At first Jessica was furious. But gradually her anger gave way to a hollow, aching sensation in the pit of her stomach. And the terrible truth sank in: She couldn't stop thinking about Jack, despite the sneaky, rotten trick he had pulled over the weekend. He was smart and fun, and just thinking about his handsome face and broad shoulders sent tingles up and down Jessica's spine. He was also a good listener and a great kisser. But what made him extra exciting was the air of mystery that surrounded him. So maybe he did have his faults. Still, Jessica had to admit that she was hooked.

She walked through the cafeteria lunch line in a daze, pictures of Jack and her moonlit night with him flashing through her mind. Then she imagined him with Lila, smiling and laughing and holding her hand. A wave of anguish swept over Jessica. What could she do? She needed some advice.

Carrying her lunch tray to the middle of the cafeteria, Jessica scanned the room for her twin. Elizabeth would help her. But there was no sign of her sister inside the crowded cafeteria. Maybe she was outside, Jessica thought. She put her tray down on the nearest table and sprinted toward the side exit that led to the outdoor eating area and the campus lawn. She wasn't hungry anyway. How could she eat at a time like this, when the man of her dreams was slipping through her fingers?

After searching the patio for her twin, Jessica ran out onto the rolling lawn. Finally, she caught sight of Elizabeth sitting under one of the great oak trees that dotted the Sweet Valley High campus. With her was Enid Rollins.

"Darn!" Jessica muttered with annoyance. How was she supposed to talk to her sister with Enid the Drip hanging around? Jessica was about to perish from heartbreak, and her twin was happily chatting away with that nerd who took up so much of her time. Count on Enid to be in the way, Jessica thought, just when she herself vitally needed her sister.

Jessica marched toward them. She could hear Enid's voice as she approached. ". . . so after the lesson, George's flying teacher gave him a demonstration of all these incredible aerial tricks."

George, George, George, Jessica thought snidely. *Doesn't that girl have anything else to talk about? She and George are like some kind of married couple.* She walked over to the tree and planted herself smack in front of Elizabeth. She stood there, while Enid continued to babble. Finally she cleared her throat as loudly as she could.

Elizabeth looked up. "Wow, Jess, that's a nasty cold you're getting," she kidded. Her blue-green eyes danced with amusement. "Maybe you'd better get it checked out."

"Liz, this is no time for jokes," Jessica declared irritably. "I don't have a cold. I was trying to get your attention."

"You're kidding!" Elizabeth deadpanned. "And I thought you'd come all the way over here to stand in front of me and shield me from the harmful rays of the sun. You know, my own personal parasol." She looked at Enid, and they both giggled.

"Elizabeth Wakefield, my entire life is being sucked right down the drain, and you're making fun of me!" Jessica coaxed a single tear down her cheek.

"Oh, Jess, I was only teasing. I didn't realize you were that upset." Elizabeth got up and wrapped a comforting arm around her sister. "What's the matter?"

"Liz, I have to talk to you," Jessica wailed. "The worst thing has happened."

"Well, I'm right here," Elizabeth said soothingly. "Talk away."

"Not here," Jessica grumbled, pulling away from her sister and shooting Enid a look of pure venom.

"Oh," Elizabeth said flatly. "Enid, I'm sorry, but will you excuse us?" she asked. "This better be a good one," she muttered to her twin as Jessica led her away. "You have this peculiar habit of needing me desperately whenever I'm with Enid."

Jessica shrugged. "Yuck. I don't know why you bother with her. Just thinking about her makes me want to curl up in a ball and go right to sleep."

"Jessica . . ." Elizabeth's voice took on a sharp edge. "Why do I have to get into this with you? Enid's a wonderful person. She's nice and intelligent, and she has a great sense of humor. And she's my best friend in the whole world."

Jessica gave a well-practiced pout.

"Besides," Elizabeth added, "I thought you told me you were in the middle of a world-class disaster. I can't imagine where you'd find the energy to pick on Enid if that were the case." She gave her twin a scrutinizing stare.

"Liz, it's the truth!" Jessica moaned. "It really is a catastrophe. You've got to tell me what to do about it."

"Jessica, maybe you ought to start by telling me what 'it' is," Elizabeth said calmly, well-used to her sister's earthshaking calamities.

"It," Jessica wailed, "is Jack."

Elizabeth shook her blond head. "I was afraid of that. Jack and Lila, right?"

Jessica swallowed hard and nodded.

"I heard the talk this morning. I only hoped, for your sake, that it wasn't true."

Jessica's tears were real now, rolling freely down her cheeks. "It is true," she said between her sobs. "I-I heard it from Lila herself." She threw herself in Elizabeth's arms and cried with abandon, taking in huge gulps of air as her sobs finally subsided.

"Jess, I know you're hurting," Elizabeth acknowledged consolingly, patting her twin on the back, "but what did you expect? You knew they had a date planned over the weekend."

"But I thought it was going to be a one-shot

71

deal." Jessica moaned. "I told you that. And now it turns out that they had some kind of 'Fantasy Island' romance."

"I know it's a tough break," Elizabeth commiserated, "but at least you found out what the guy's really all about before you got too involved."

"But I *am* involved!" Jessica sank down on the grass and rested her head between her hands. "I may even be in love with him!"

"Jess, how could you be? You've gone out with him exactly once." Elizabeth sat down next to her sister.

Jessica whipped her head around and threw Elizabeth a ferocious glare. "Are you saying it's impossible? How many dates did it take for you to fall in love with Todd? You know as well as I do that after one kiss you were totally and completely head over heels."

Elizabeth couldn't deny that. And her face lit up as she remembered that first searching kiss. But the smile on her lips vanished almost instantly. "Todd wasn't seeing anyone but me, Jessica. If he had been, the romance would have been over before it started. You should know not to get any more involved with Jack. As far as I'm concerned, the sooner you forget about him, the better."

"Oh, I get it," Jessica retorted. "Todd's the good guy, and Jack's the bad guy. Look, I was counting on you for advice. Now what kind of help is that?"

"Advice on how to win Jack over? Jess, I could be wrong, but I have a feeling that you're only going to be hurt even worse if you don't start getting that guy out of your system right this second."

Jessica stood up abruptly, her eyes like aqua ice. "Not only *could* you be wrong, but you *are* wrong, Liz. I want Jack, and I'm going to get him, with or without your help. And next time I think about coming to you for advice, I'd darn well better think again." She marched off in a huff, leaving her sister to stare after her.

Perhaps Jessica *could* win Jack over, Elizabeth mused. It was seldom that her twin wanted something and didn't get it. But she couldn't shake the nagging suspicion that what Jessica got was going to be more than she had bargained for. As she watched Jessica storm across the Sweet Valley lawn, Elizabeth could only cross her fingers and pray that her hunch was wrong.

Seven

Elizabeth was on the living-room couch on Tuesday night, studying her French idioms, when Jessica breezed into the room.

"How does this outfit look?" she asked, turning slowly as she modeled her crimson sweater-dress, with the buttons running all the way down the back, and her flat-soled black sandals. Her hair was brushed to a shine, and one strand was woven into a tiny side braid.

"What's the occasion? Wait—let me guess," said Elizabeth, noting her sister's radiant smile. "He called, right?" There was no question as to who "he" was.

Jessica nodded happily as she sat down beside Elizabeth. "He's on his way over right now to pick me up. We're going to see a showing of *Help!* over at the Somerville Quad."

Elizabeth put her French book down on the coffee table. "What did he say about Lila?"

Jessica's smile was gone in a flash. "Did you have to bring that up just now?" she snapped.

"If I didn't know you better, I'd think you were purposely trying to ruin my good mood." A sullen look on her face, she sank down on the couch next to her sister.

Elizabeth's cheeks turned scarlet. "Jess, I didn't mean to—um—I figured—well—I just assumed that if you were seeing Jack, he must have given you a good explanation of what was going on."

"Nope. And I didn't ask him." Jessica's defiant tone clearly said, "Case closed."

But Elizabeth was persistent. "Well, are you going to?"

Jessica rolled her eyes. "What are you, Liz, my mother or something? Yes, I do plan to ask him. Largely to get you off my back."

"Good. I think you should," Elizabeth said coolly, ignoring Jessica's biting remark. "I simply don't want to see you get hurt, that's all. And I really do hope there's a reasonable explanation for all of this. You know how much I want you to be happy."

Jessica continued to scowl.

"It's true. Come on, Jess, can't you just smile?"

Jessica shook her head, refusing to look in her sister's direction.

"Pretty please?" Elizabeth reached over and tickled Jessica.

Jessica's sober face gave way almost instantly. "No—stop—Liz," she said, giggling. "Too—too ticklish," she gasped. She struggled out of her sister's reach and then pounced back with a tickle of her own.

In less time than it takes to say "uncle," the tickle fight was in full swing. Both girls were laughing so hard, their stomachs ached, but neither showed the slightest sign of giving up. It might have gone on like that all night if the doorbell hadn't rung—just as Elizabeth was getting in a superb tickle under her twin's left arm.

Suddenly Jessica jumped up and started running her fingers through her hair. "It must be Jack!" she exclaimed.

"It could be Todd, too," Elizabeth said, catching her breath. "He said he might stop over to study tonight."

A look of alarm crossed Jessica's face. "You're kidding!"

"No. Why?" Elizabeth was puzzled.

"Well, what if he sees Jack coming to get me? I don't want anyone to know about us but you!"

The doorbell sounded again, this time with several sharp, persistent rings. Elizabeth moved to answer it. "Jess, don't worry," she said. "Your secret's as safe with Todd as it is with me. You have my word. But you know, eventually people are going to see you together."

"Well, let's hope that by the time that happens, everything is official between us," Jessica said as she straightened her dress. "And that a

certain friend of mine, who shall remain name-
less, is out of the picture."

Elizabeth's brow furrowed slightly. She
refrained from commenting, however, as she
pulled the front door open.

"Ah, the gates finally open," Todd said, giving Elizabeth a quick kiss as he stepped inside.
"Jack and I were beginning to think we were
going to be staring at your front door all night."

Jack was indeed right behind Todd, standing
on the Wakefields' doorstep. "Jack, come in,"
Elizabeth invited politely.

"Hi!" Jessica sang out, running over and putting her arm around him.

But after all the hellos were said, there was a
silence. It wasn't the best combination of people,
Elizabeth reflected. In addition to her own wari-
ness about Jack, her sister and Todd had a rather
rocky history. Add that to the fact that Todd
probably had no idea why Jack was there and
that Jessica was none too pleased at the prospect
of having him find out. As for Jack, who knew
what he was thinking? Elizabeth couldn't get any
sort of a handle on what he was like under his
perfect J. Press wardrobe and his upper-crust
manners.

She looked at him out of the corner of her eye.
He was as handsome as he had been at Lila's
pool party, but on more careful examination,
Elizabeth saw that his deep-set eyes were puffy
and ringed with red.

"Jack, are you feeling all right?" she asked, breaking the silence. "You look a little under the weather."

"I think he looks great," Jessica said defensively.

"I didn't mean it like that." Elizabeth sighed, feeling the tension level shoot up another notch.

"It's OK," Jack said. "I did just come from the pool at the community center. The chlorine sometimes irritates my eyes." The tension level sank a bit.

"Oh, you work out at the community center?" Todd asked. "I go there to shoot baskets a lot. Maybe I'll see you there. I don't use the pool much, though. I guess I'm a landlubber at heart."

"Well, as they say in French, *chacun à son goût*," Elizabeth declared, testing out one of the new idioms she had been studying. Her remark went over like a lead weight.

"Liz, would you mind telling us normal folk what that's supposed to mean?" Jessica demanded.

"*Ma chère* Jessica," Elizabeth said, laughing, "if you'd done your homework for Ms. Dalton's class, you'd know. It means 'to each his own.' Or 'her own,' as the case may be."

"Yeah, well, I could go for a seat in the Somerville movie theater, myself," Jessica said. She linked her arm through Jack's. "Have a fun

78

evening, study-bugs," she said as she led Jack out the door.

"Wow! What's going on with those two?" Todd asked a moment after they had left. "I thought he and Lila were hot and heavy."

Elizabeth shrugged helplessly as she settled back down on the couch. "Who knows? If Jess has her way, they won't be for long."

Todd let out a low, long whistle. "But Lila's her friend!" he exclaimed, as he and Elizabeth walked into the living room and sat down on the couch. "If that isn't just like Jessica!"

Elizabeth bit down hard on her lip. Her boyfriend's often stormy feelings about Jessica were the one source of irritation in their relationship.

"Doesn't your sister stop at anything?" Todd asked.

"Todd Wilkins! What's that supposed to mean?" Elizabeth crossed her arms angrily. "So perhaps Jessica *has* gone a tiny bit overboard with this latest crush. It's no reason for you to start picking on her again!"

"Liz, listen, I'm sorry. I'm not picking on her. Really. But the whole thing doesn't seem right, somehow."

Elizabeth sighed. "I wish I could argue with you, Todd, but the truth is, I feel kind of nervous about this situation, too. Not through any fault of Jessica's, though," she added hastily, still miffed because of Todd's remark concerning her sister. "But I have a funny feeling about Jack. To begin with, he's playing an awfully dangerous game with Jess and Lila. You know it's going to end badly for someone—or maybe for all of them." She shook her head. "And then there's this business about Jessica's keeping their relationship a secret. She hasn't said as much, but I suspect that she's simply afraid of losing out to Lila and doesn't want to be humiliated if things don't work out. Frankly, I can't even understand why she'd bother with a guy who made her feel like that."

"Maybe he's got some special charm that you and I don't see," Todd commented, "but to me he seemed—I don't know—kind of out of it just now. Know what I mean?" Todd moved closer to Elizabeth and put his arm around her shoulder.

"Uh-huh," Elizabeth agreed. "He seemed so different from the friendly, energetic guy at Lila's party. You know, he didn't even respond when I made that comment in French—and he's supposed to speak fluent French." Elizabeth paused. "But maybe he's just worn out," she concluded. She always tried to believe the best about people. "He does work awfully hard all week."

"Maybe you're right," Todd responded, stroking Elizabeth's hair. "But let's not worry about him anymore." He pulled her closer. "I've got better things in mind."

As Todd's lips met Elizabeth's in a slow, sweet kiss, Jack was temporarily forgotten.

"How about if I got us some popcorn and a couple of soft drinks?" Jessica suggested, once she and Jack had gotten settled in the center row of the movie theater. Certainly someone as big on independence as Jack would go for a girl who believed in sharing the expenses of a date.

"Oh, let me get it," Jack offered, starting to get out of his seat.

"Please. I'd like to do the buying," Jessica insisted, putting a restraining hand on his arm as she reached for her shoulder bag. Being on the giving as well as the receiving end was more Elizabeth's style than hers, but if Jack liked people who stood on their own two feet, that was what he would get.

Jessica fumbled around inside her bag for her wallet. She could almost hear her sister's voice saying, "You know, Jess, it's only fair that the guy get treated sometimes, too." Well, maybe Elizabeth knew a thing or two. Jessica's fingers found her keys, her address book, and various items of makeup as she searched for her money. She looked inside her bag. A pencil, a dried-up felt-tipped pen with no cap, a crinkled-up note that Cara had passed her in study hall that day, but no wallet. She looked again: no sign of it.

"Oh, my god!" she cried. "My money—it's gone!"

"Are you sure?" Jack asked, his forehead creased.

Jessica jumped up in a panic and dumped the contents of her bag onto the fabric-covered seat. Her wallet was not there, nor was it on the floor, or anywhere around where she was sitting.

"How much was in there?" Jack asked, poking around under their chairs.

"A ten-dollar bill and a few ones and some change," Jessica wailed.

Jack took Jessica's hand and gave it a reassuring squeeze. "You probably left it at home," he consoled her. "I bet you find it right on your bedroom floor, or something. Don't worry. It'll turn up."

Jessica looked doubtful.

"It will. I promise," Jack said. "Meanwhile, I'll get the popcorn. You just relax and get ready to enjoy the movie." He left his seat and made his way down the theater aisle.

But Jessica couldn't relax. She searched frantically for the next few minutes, scouring her entire row, and the rows in front and back of her as well. "Excuse me," she muttered, squeezing past the enormous woman who had the seat next to hers. She got down on her hands and knees and peered under a few more chairs.

At that second, Jack returned, with a large tub of popcorn, two 7-Ups, and a box of Raisinettes.

Immediately Jessica sprang up, embarrassed at being caught on her hands and knees on the sticky cinema floor. She could feel her cheeks flush.

But Jack, ever the gentleman, simply put down the refreshments and helped Jessica to her feet. "Jess—we'll find your money later, but there's nothing we can do right now." He steered her back to her seat. "So forget about it for the moment. Doctor's orders, OK?" He took Jessica's face in his hands and gently tilted it upward so that her gaze met his. "OK, Jess?" he repeated.

Jessica stared up at his handsome, fine-featured face. Suddenly her lost wallet didn't seem so important anymore. "OK, Dr. Jack," she murmured as he slipped one arm down around her shoulder.

True to her word, once the movie began, Jessica forgot everything, except Jack's nearness. As the Beatles frolicked on the screen, she let her hand graze his leg and come to rest just above his knee. Perhaps this was going to be a good evening after all!

"So what did you think?" Jack asked as they were walking to the car after the movie was over.

"Really good," Jessica said. "Can you imagine what it must have been like to see the Beatles in concert? Wow, if only I had been around back then!"

"Yeah, they were definitely a terrific group," Jack commented as he unlocked the car. "But you have to admit there are some hot groups now, too. Like the Police. Boy, do they put on a good show!"

"You mean you've heard them live?" Jessica asked once they were settled inside the Rambler.

"Yup. They played two nights at the Hartford Coliseum, not too far from where I prepped. The second night some of my buddies and I went down to see them. It was incredible."

Jack proceeded to launch into a detailed description of the concert, but Jessica was only half-listening. She was focusing on more important things—like the clue Jack had inadvertently dropped about his background. Hartford. Jessica thought that was in Connecticut. And Jack had said he'd gone to prep school near there. Well, that confirmed it. Jack really was someone worth knowing. The very best boarding schools in the country were in New England, and all the most important families sent their sons and daughters there. Yet again Jessica found herself wondering, as she had so many times during the past week, who Jack really was.

She imagined herself on his arm, being given a tour of the palatial mansion he called home. (For of course, after Jack had his taste of independence, he would be welcomed back to his family with open arms.) "This is the lady Jessica," he would say, as he introduced her to all the servants. To his family she would simply be "Jessica, my most cherished companion." Jessica would give a regal nod of her head as the introductions were made. Naturally, there would be a great feast prepared in her honor, one that would put Lila's expensive buffets to shame. . . .

Lila. Jessica felt the cold sting of reality as she remembered her rival. There wasn't going to be a feast or tour of any mansion as long as Lila was in the picture. Jessica had to say something to Jack. Now. She studied his profile and took a deep breath as she summoned up her nerve.

"So then they came out for another encore," Jack was saying, wrapping up his blow-by-blow description of the Police concert. "And they played my favorite song, 'Every Breath You Take.' Jess, you should have been there."

"Oh, Jack, I'll bet you say that to all the girls." Jessica's joking tone was spiked with a danger-ous dash of seriousness.

"What other girls?" Jack was the picture of innocence.

"Oh, come on. Everybody's heard about you and Lila." Jessica's blue-green eyes studied Jack intently, but there was no sign of a reaction. "Not that I don't think there must be a perfectly good explanation for your behavior," she added, giving Jack an opening for exactly the kind of response she wanted to hear.

"What behavior?" Jack made a turn onto the winding road that led up to Miller's Point, a scenic overlook favored by young couples who usually had no intention of looking at the view.

Jessica could feel her anger taking hold. Why was Jack engaging her in this transparent game of verbal cat and mouse? "I suppose you brought Lila up here, too," she blurted out as the plateau of Miller's Point came into sight ahead of them.

"Jessica, Lila and I are just friends. I don't know where you got any other idea."

"Are you telling me that you *didn't* spend the entire weekend with her?" Jessica grilled.

Jack pulled the Rambler up to the overlook, joining a half-dozen or so other cars that were already parked there.

"Well—I was with her," Jack hedged, "but—"

"But what?" By now Jessica's tone was accusing.

"Look, Jessica!" Though Jack's voice was low, those two words came out with the force of an explosion. For the merest fraction of a second, Jack's face grew frighteningly fierce, and Jessica suddenly felt afraid. But her fear disappeared in an instant, as Jack gave his head a hard shake and his expression softened. "Jessica." He pronounced her name gently this time. "I did ask Lila out for Friday night. You know, she invited me to that party when she hardly knew me. It was my way of reciprocating."

Jack was telling Jessica exactly what she had told Elizabeth the previous week. She felt her anger give way a bit.

"And then she invited me to spend Saturday on her sailfish," Jack explained.

"And you went?" Jessica was back on the offensive.

"Jess, haven't you ever accepted an invitation to do something with a guy who's just your friend?"

Jessica was caught on this point. Just a few days before, Ken Matthews had taken her waterskiing. It had been a terrific day, but, Jessica had to admit to herself, a day without romantic expectations on either her part or Ken's.

"I suppose I have been in that situation once or twice," Jessica allowed. "But what about Sunday? Lila said she saw you then, also."

"That's true." Jack looked Jessica directly in the eye. "But it wasn't intentional. We ran into each other at the mall and ended up having lunch together."

"And you think I'm going to believe that?"

"I hope you will." Jack reached over and took one of Jessica's hands in his. "Because that's what really happened."

Doubt continued to color Jessica's face.

"Please trust me," Jack whispered. "You're the girl I want."

Jessica turned toward him. His strong chin and chiseled cheekbones were illuminated by moonlight spilling through the Rambler windows. "I want to trust you," Jessica responded carefully. "But I know that Lila's convinced you're interested in her."

"Well, then, she's mistaken. I like her as a friend. You can certainly understand that, Jessica. After all, she's a friend of yours, too. But my feelings end there." Jack's expression grew grim. "I guess I have no choice but to tell her."

"When?" Jessica demanded.

"Friday. I'll see her Friday. And I'll tell her what I just told you."

The corners of Jessica's lips turned up, and a smile spread across her face. "Oh, Jack, I knew you would!" Suddenly she was as sweet as pecan pie.

From then on, the night only got better. Jessica never did find her wallet, but by the end of the evening she felt that she had gained something far more important—Jack's undivided affection.

A job well done, she congratulated herself silently as she and Jack shared one last, lingering kiss on her doorstep. *Chalk up another win for Jessica Wakefield.*

Eight

Finished! Elizabeth thought with satisfaction as she put the final touches on the latest issue of *The Oracle*. It was Thursday night, and the paper was pasted up and ready to go to the printers. Penny would be proud of her!

She leaned back in her chair and looked around the *Oracle* office. Empty, except for her. Even the staff members who had stayed late to help out had long since gone home.

Outside the office windows, the sky was a deep, purplish-blue. Elizabeth stretched her arms above her head. She felt tired but happy— enveloped by a real sense of accomplishment. She couldn't wait to see all her friends and the rest of the kids at school poring over the pages she had painstakingly supervised and put together.

She thumbed through her work one last time and then carefully put all of it in Penny's desk drawer and locked the drawer with a tiny key, on loan from Penny. The key hung around her neck on a slender white ribbon, along with her own key to the *Oracle* office.

She stood up and gathered her things together, realizing, for the first time all evening, how hungry she was. An ice-cream sundae at Casey's Place on the way home would just about do the trick. Elizabeth could picture her mother telling her that a sundae was no substitute for a real dinner, but she could almost taste the creamy, homemade ice cream, smothered in hot fudge sauce. Besides, after all her hard work, she deserved a treat.

Elizabeth took a final look around her to make sure everything was in its proper place, shut off the overhead lights, and let herself out of the room. As she was pulling the door closed, she bumped smack into someone directly in back of her. Muffling a cry, she whirled around to see who it was. In the dim light, cast by the illuminated emergency exit sign near the staircase, stood Penny Ayala's little sister, Tina, looking every bit as startled as Elizabeth herself.

"Tina! You scared me!" Elizabeth exclaimed. "What are you doing here? It must be almost nine o'clock."

"Quarter to," Tina corrected, her voice a little shaky.

"What's up? Penny didn't send you over here with any last-minute instructions, did she?" *Just when I thought I had finished*, Elizabeth thought.

"No, Penny didn't ask me to come," Tina said.

Elizabeth was relieved. "Well, did you want to speak to me?"

"Not exactly," Tina hedged. "In fact, I didn't expect to find anyone here at this hour."

"Oh?" Elizabeth's expression was puzzled. She felt as if she were playing a game of twenty questions with Tina to find out what she was doing here. Yet she had seemed so friendly and open the last time they had met.

Suddenly Elizabeth noticed Tina sneaking her right hand behind her back. But she didn't do it quite smoothly enough to escape Elizabeth's detection. In the second it took her to take her hand out of view, Elizabeth caught sight of what Tina was holding: several black-and-white photographs! Elizabeth instantly realized what Tina was doing lurking outside the *Oracle* office and why she insisted on being so secretive.

"It's you!" Elizabeth gasped. "You're the phantom photographer, aren't you?"

There was an anxious expression on Tina's plump face. "You won't tell, will you?"

"Well, Penny did give me orders to find out who was taking those pictures. . . ."

"No!" Tina's cry rang through the empty hallway. "You mustn't tell her!"

"Tina, I don't understand what you're so nervous about," Elizabeth said gently. "Everybody loves your pictures."

A ghost of a smile flickered across Tina's face, but it didn't stay long.

"Especially your sister," Elizabeth added.

"Really?" Tina sounded surprised.

"Really," Elizabeth assured her. "She told me she wants to put the phantom photographer on staff."

Tina's smile returned, but only for a moment. "Oh, she won't feel that way once she finds out it's me," she lamented, the corners of her mouth turning down.

"Why not?" Elizabeth shook her head in confusion. "I've always known Penny to stick to her word."

"Maybe to everyone else, but I'm just her unimportant, nothing baby sister." Tina swallowed hard. "When I was little, everyone was always saying, 'Penny did this terrific thing,' or 'Penny got that special award,' or 'Watch Penny do it. She's a real pro.' And nothing's really changed all that much. Penny's still the impressive one—the big editor of the paper, the straight-A student headed for the best college." Tears welled up in Tina's eyes. "There wouldn't be room for both of us on *The Oracle*. I just can't compete with her, so why bother trying?"

Elizabeth put a hand on Tina's shoulder. "It's not a matter of competition, Tina. Penny's the editor of the paper, not the photographer. You'd be working *together*, as a team."

Tina seemed to consider this for a minute. "No," she said. "Penny wouldn't be able to take me seriously. Her freshman sister on the paper with all you juniors and seniors? It just wouldn't work."

"What makes you so sure?" Elizabeth queried. "I think Penny recognizes talent when she sees it."

"Yeah, as long as it's not mine," Tina replied. "That's why I started leaving all those photos anonymously."

"Tina, think of it this way." Elizabeth gave it one more try. "Penny has told me, flat out, that she thinks the phantom photos are great and she wants the person who took them to be a staff photographer. When she finds out that person is you, it might make her take a really serious look at you—as a talented person with something to offer, not as Tina, her little sister."

Tina was silent for a long time. Finally she nodded slowly. "You're very persuasive, Liz."

"Then you'll do it? You'll tell Penny you took the pictures?" Elizabeth asked.

Tina immediately went white.

"How about if I tell her?" Elizabeth quickly amended, afraid of having Tina back out.

Tina smiled, and this time the smile remained. "You don't mind?" she asked gratefully.

"Not at all. I think it could be good for both of you to work together."

Still clutching her latest photos in her hand, Tina exuberantly threw her arms around Elizabeth. "Liz, thank you so much. If I can ever do any favors for you . . ."

Elizabeth laughed happily. "As a matter of fact, you can start by showing me those pictures you're holding. I'm dying of curiosity!"

"Sure!" Tina responded, handing Elizabeth three pictures. "I decided to shoot a roll of film on after-school activities. These are my favorites from that batch. But it's going to be awfully hard to see anything under that." She motioned to the dim exit sign.

Elizabeth fingered the ribbon around her neck and grasped the key to the *Oracle* office. She unlocked the door, stepped inside, and switched the lights back on. "Better get used to this place," she joked as Tina followed her into the room. "From now on you're going to be spending a lot of time here!"

"I hope so," Tina answered.

Elizabeth sat down in the nearest chair and glanced at the first picture. It had been taken in the new game room at Dairi Burger and showed Allen Walters, the school math and science whiz, and a photographer for *The Oracle*, engaged in an intense battle with a video game. The next photo was of DeeDee Gordon, teetering on her surfboard, on the verge of being toppled by a monster of a wave. "What an action shot!" Elizabeth's voice rang with enthusiasm. "These are great, Tina." She flashed Tina an encouraging smile as she put the first two pictures on the desktop next to her. Then she turned her attention to the final shot. What she saw made her gasp.

Tina had obviously gone out to the airfield to take photos of the students in the flying class. In the photo Elizabeth now held in her hand, Tina had caught Robin Wilson and George Warren against a backdrop of small planes. And they were locked in a heated embrace!

Later that night Elizabeth sat in the Wakefields' study, staring glumly at the television set. On the screen, Humphrey Bogart starred in her all-time favorite old movie, *The Maltese Falcon*. But she was barely watching it, her head swimming instead with images of George and Robin. What would happen if Enid found out? She'd be absolutely crushed. As her best friend, it was Elizabeth's responsibility to protect her, wasn't it? Or perhaps it was her duty to make sure Enid wasn't kept in the dark.

Elizabeth battled with herself, trying to decide what to do, as Bogie, playing the detective Sam Spade, followed the elusive trail of the much-sought-after falcon statue.

One thing was certain—the picture Tina had taken would remain a secret, seen only by Elizabeth and the photographer herself. They had agreed on that after Elizabeth had explained the sticky situation to Tina.

"Oh, dear," Tina had moaned. "And I thought I was taking a happy, romantic picture."

"Don't blame yourself," Elizabeth had consoled her. "These things do happen." *But why do they have to happen to someone as sweet and good as Enid?* she had lamented silently.

Elizabeth continued to wonder about this as Sam Spade tried to unravel his own mystery on the TV in front of her. *It just isn't fair. Enid deserves better than this.*

Suddenly Jessica waltzed into the study and plopped down next to her sister. "Ooh, Humphrey Bogart. Great." She tucked a pillow under her head and put her feet up on the little glass table in front of her. "What movie is this?" she asked, poking Elizabeth in the ribs.

"*The Maltese Falcon,*" Elizabeth replied in a monotone.

Jessica turned her head toward her twin with a sharp motion and regarded her quizzically.

"You sound like you're about to die, Liz. What's the matter? I thought you loved this movie."

"I do."

"So why the long face?"

"Oh, it's nothing." *Nothing, that is, that I want anyone else to know about until the situation is resolved,* she thought.

Jessica shrugged. "Suit yourself," she declared, turning back to Bogart, who was now embroiled in some heavy onscreen wheeling and dealing. But a few seconds later, she turned back to Elizabeth. "Is it Todd?" she demanded.

"Is what Todd? Jessica, I told you, nothing's wrong." Elizabeth forced a weak smile for her sister's benefit.

"OK. If we can't talk about *you*, maybe we should talk about *me*," Jessica proposed. "Don't you want to know how my evening was?"

Elizabeth sighed. She really needed to be alone, to think through Enid and George's messy situation in as clear and logical a manner as possible. But if she excused herself right now, Jessica would know for certain that something was up. Then Elizabeth would have no peace whatsoever, until her twin discovered what it was. "All right," Elizabeth gave in. "How was your evening?"

"I thought you would never ask," Jessica said dramatically. "It was amazing! Jack and I had the best time."

Elizabeth raised one eyebrow. "Jack again?"

Jessica nodded happily. "We took the most beautiful drive up and down the coast highway. And we stopped at this cozy little clam bar overlooking the ocean."

"Oh, yeah, I know that place. Up by Marpa Heights. Todd took me there once. It's an awfully romantic spot, isn't it?" Elizabeth commented, remembering a special evening of her own there.

Jessica grew starry-eyed. "Every place is romantic when I'm with Jack. And pretty soon he'll be all mine," she added contentedly.

"Tomorrow night he's going to level with Lila. Then it'll be him and me—from then on."

Elizabeth studied Jessica's exhilarated, radiant face. Maybe she'd been wrong about Jack. She hoped so. After all, she reasoned, how bad could he be, if he was making her sister so happy? "I'm glad for you, Jess," she said sincerely.

"You are? No kidding?" Jessica's blue-green eyes shone brightly.

"You look so satisfied. How could I not approve?"

"Liz, you're my favorite sister in the whole world!" Jessica threw her arms around her twin.

"I'm your only sister, you nut." She rumpled Jessica's hair playfully. It was good to see her twin in such high spirits, Elizabeth thought. She made a decision, then and there, to be more open toward Jack. Anyone who cared about her sister deserved as much.

By the time she got ready for bed that evening, Elizabeth's mood was at least somewhat improved. Her concern about Enid and George was still unresolved, but her fears about Jessica had been laid to rest. She was glad she had been wrong about Jack. By the next evening he would have set the record straight with Lila, and her twin would be one of the happiest girls in Sweet Valley.

Nine

"Lila," Jack crooned in her ear as they sipped wine in the Fowlers' outdoor sculpture garden beneath the brilliant stars, "I think I'm falling in love with you!"

"Oh, Jack. I love you, too!" Lila snuggled as close to Jack as she could and lay her head against his chest. She wished she could stay this way forever, nestled in Jack's strong arms, breathing in his masculine scent and the sweetness of the night air. *Nothing could be more perfect*, she thought.

"Every time I see you, I feel closer and closer to you," Jack murmured, tracing the contours of her face with his fingertips.

"Me, too." Lila's voice was filled with tenderness. "I thought I was as happy as I could be with you last night. But this evening I'm even more in love with you. It just keeps getting better." She brushed her lips across his. "And better."

Jack took a delicate sip of his Château Lafite-

Rothschild, compliments of the Fowlers' superlative wine cellar. George Fowler was away on business again, and Lila had taken the opportunity to help herself to one of her father's best wines. She wasn't old enough to drink, and her father severely prohibited it, but she figured he'd never miss one little bottle. Besides, Jack was more than suitably impressed by the vintage label. It was worth the risk of being found out when her father returned.

"Mmm," Jack said, swirling the wine in his glass and savoring its bouquet, "this wine is almost as exquisite as you are. But not quite." He put his glass back down on the little table next to him and cupped Lila's face in his large, strong hands. "You're so beautiful," he murmured. "Lila, I thought I'd never say this to anyone, but I could imagine spending the rest of my life with you."

Lila's eyes opened wide in joyful astonishment. "You really mean that?" she asked incredulously.

"I want to be with you forever," Jack whispered, kissing her softly several times. "You're the only girl for me."

"And you're my only guy," Lila returned passionately. "Always." As she uttered the last word, her voice dropped, and she trembled with elation. Always. For eternity. Could it really be true? She and Jack, together forever. The notion set her mind spinning. She was in a state of dizzy euphoria.

Theirs would be the engagement of the century. For starters, there'd be a party to end all parties, heralding their love with the grandest, most elegant celebration Southern California had ever seen. Everybody who was anybody would toast the happy young couple; reporters would snap pictures of the spectacular event; and presiding over the festivities would be Lila herself, the envy of every girl in Sweet Valley, not to mention everywhere else.

"Yes, always," Jack was saying. "The two of us. Some day I want you to be my wife."

"Oh, Jack, I want that, too!" Lila thought she might faint from sheer bliss. She could just see the headlines of *The Sweet Valley News* now: "Miss Lila Fowler, daughter of computer-chip millionaire, is engaged . . ."

"Of course it will have to remain a secret, for now." Jack's voice broke into her thoughts.

"It will?" Lila's mood of jubilation suddenly took an unpleasant detour. "But why?" She pulled free of his grasp and shot him a questioning look.

"Lila, I simply can't chance having my father find out where I am." He paused for a moment. "Let's keep the news between ourselves, all right?"

Some of the fire in Lila's eyes had died down. No big engagement party? No ring shimmering on her finger to flaunt to everyone at Sweet Valley High?

"You know, if this got leaked to the press somehow, I'd be in big trouble," Jack added. "They'd jump on the story in a second."

"They would?" All of Lila's attention shifted back to Jack immediately. Who was he, that the press would so eagerly snatch up any piece of information on him? A very important young man, that was who. Instantly the fire in her eyes was rekindled. "Jack, I won't tell a soul," Lila promised. "All that really matters is you and me."

"That's what I want to hear." Jack reached for Lila's hand. "And I propose we name a star in honor of our love. That one," he pointed, "because it's the brightest in the sky. From now on, every time I look at it, I'll think of this wonderful night."

"Oh, Jack, how romantic."

"And tomorrow night," he added, "we'll have a special celebration—just the two of us, OK?"

Tomorrow. Sunday night. The night her father was due home. Once again, Lila came back down to earth with an excruciating thud. Jack and her father had still not met. And engagement or no engagement, Astor, Du Pont, or Vanderbilt though he might be, Jack would still rate nothing more in her father's eyes at this time than the title of rebellious son. Lila realized now that her pact of secrecy with Jack was as vital to her as it was to him.

"Jack," she said nervously, "I don't think we can meet here tomorrow. My father—he's having a little dinner party," she fabricated weakly, crossing the fingers of her free hand behind her back. How could she tell the boy she was engaged to that she didn't want him to meet her father?

But Jack was undaunted. "Then we'll just have to meet at my house," he said.

Lila was bathed in a sense of relief. The problem had been avoided. At least for now. "Your house sounds great," she said, laying her head against Jack's chest once more and giving in to the consuming pleasure of being next to him.

She'd worry about her father some other time. With the stars blanketing the sky and her arms around the most handsome boy she'd ever met, this evening was too special to be anything less than one-hundred-percent fabulous. Lila wanted to remember it always, a night of unqualified perfection—the night she became the fiancée of Sweet Valley's mystery prince.

But in a house in the valley below the Fowlers' sprawling estate, Elizabeth Wakefield's night was going as badly as Lila's was going well. Her date with Todd had been blemished by constant thoughts of Enid, George, and Robin, and as

103

hard as she'd tried, she couldn't fool Todd into believing that nothing was wrong.

When he'd insisted on knowing what was troubling her, she couldn't tell him that, either. It wasn't that she couldn't count on her boyfriend to keep any secret she told him; on the contrary, she trusted him completely. But if Enid didn't know about George and Robin, Elizabeth didn't feel she had the right to tell anyone else about them. Even Todd.

She knew things would have been much easier if she could have told him. She desperately needed to talk to someone about the whole messy business. Yet it just wouldn't have been fair to Enid.

Elizabeth had finally said she wasn't feeling well—which was true, in a way—and had come home early. Now she lay in bed, tossing restlessly and trying to decide what she could possibly do to help Enid. Should she talk to her friend? Let her know what she had seen? There was the first problem. Elizabeth hadn't actually seen anything. Except a photograph. And how much ought she to assume from that? Maybe there was a legitimate explanation for Robin and George's embrace. Perhaps it had happened only once and was no more than a quick, friendly kiss. It hadn't looked that way to Elizabeth when she'd studied Tina's snapshot, but her judgment had been uncharacteristically unreliable lately. After all, Jack, the guy she'd had so little trust in, was making her twin sister wonderfully happy. No, she couldn't rely on her intuition alone. That was the second problem. And even if there *was* something going on between George and Robin, was it Elizabeth's business to interfere? That was the third problem.

In the end, Elizabeth came to the conclusion that there was only one thing to do: She would have to go out to the airfield the next afternoon, when the flying licenses were to be awarded, and speak with George and Robin herself. They were the only people who could lay her fears to rest—or confirm the awful reality of what she suspected.

The rest of the night was spent tossing and turning in dread anticipation of the next day's confrontation. Facing George and Robin was not going to be easy. Over and over, Elizabeth played out in her mind every possible variation of the conversation she would have with them. Several times she considered backing out. But doing nothing would have to be the worst agony of all.

Elizabeth finally fell into a light sleep, but it was filled with images of Enid and George, George and Robin, Enid and Robin; and in one particularly disturbing dream, even Enid's old boyfriend, Ronnie Edwards, made a surreal cameo appearance.

Elizabeth was relieved when she finally awoke

to the smells of fresh coffee and frying bacon wafting upstairs to her bedroom to signal the start of a new day. Her fitful sleep had left her more drained than refreshed, and she was grateful to be able to get up and leave her bed behind.

At brunch, she let Jessica do most of the talking. And Jessica seized the opportunity to tell her parents all about Jack and how wonderful he was.

Elizabeth stretched the meal out as long as she could, refilling her coffee cup several times, then lingering over the dishes, which she volunteered to do without Jessica's help. But finally there was nothing left to stand between her and the task ahead of her. She found her mother in the study, working on some sketches for a design project, and asked if she could borrow the Fiat.

"I don't see why not," Alice Wakefield said, looking up from her work. "What do you need it for?"

Elizabeth avoided her mother's blue-eyed gaze. "I want to watch the flying class receive their pilots' licenses at noon. It's the last day of the program, so I thought I might cover it for *The Oracle*. You know, as a follow-up to the article I had Robin Wilson write."

As with the excuse she had given Todd the previous night for going home early, this was at least partially true—but the truth was twisted and stretched thin. Jessica was a master of this trick, but Elizabeth, who firmly believed in telling the whole truth and nothing but the truth, stared uncomfortably at the floor.

"Of course you can take the car," her mother said again, "but are you sure you're OK, Liz? You hardly said a word at breakfast."

"I'm fine, Mom." Elizabeth tried to sound convincing. But as she climbed into the little red convertible and turned on the ignition, she felt weighed down by a stifling sense of foreboding.

She followed the winding road out to the airfield almost automatically, her thoughts on less pleasant things than the lush, hilly vista rolling by the car windows. Her stomach did somersaults as the countryside eventually began to level off and small planes, low overhead, indicated that the airfield was not far away.

A few minutes later, Elizabeth steered the Fiat into the parking lot near the edge of the runway. As she got out of the car, she could see that the awards ceremony had already begun. A man in an aviator's uniform was calling out names, and one by one the new pilots stepped up to him and received their licenses to fly. Elizabeth walked closer and could make out the familiar faces of some of her classmates amidst the group that was gathered in front of her. She scanned the crowd. Suddenly her focus riveted itself on one particular face—smiling, beautiful Robin Wilson. And at her side was George Warren.

Elizabeth's first reaction was panic. *Oh, no, it's true*, she thought, on the verge of turning and running away as quickly as she could. But somewhere inside her a little voice said, "No, you don't. You came here to talk to George and Robin, not to jump to any conclusions." After all they weren't doing anything wrong. They were just standing next to each other. That didn't prove a thing. Especially since it appeared that the students' names were being called in alphabetical order. Elizabeth saw a spark of hope and grabbed on to it. Warren, Wilson . . . yes, there was a reason why they were together.

But a few stress-filled minutes later, her hope was extinguished. Elizabeth watched from a distance as George stepped up to receive his license, followed by Robin. The congratulations they exchanged immediately afterward were decidedly more than just friendly. Elizabeth would have liked to have melted into the ground. Instead she discreetly waited until they stopped embracing and then went over to where they stood.

George spotted her first. "Liz!" he exclaimed in a startled voice. He and Robin exchanged quick, nervous glances and jumped apart hastily, putting a few inches of space between them. But it was clearly a pointless gesture.

Robin hung her head in embarrassment. "You've been watching for a while, haven't you?" she asked, directing her question more at the tops of her shoes, it seemed, than at Elizabeth.

"I'm afraid so." Elizabeth toyed with her blond ponytail, obviously as ill at ease as the two of them were. Taking a deep breath, she plunged into an explanation of the photo Tina Ayala had shown her and how she'd felt she ought to check out the facts before making any assumptions.

"I kept hoping it wasn't true," she said, "but now that I know it is—well—I don't have any idea what to say." She spread her hands in the air helplessly. Robin had always been Elizabeth's friend, and she had spent so many wonderful times with George—at the beach with Enid and Todd, double-dating over dinner or dancing at the Beach Disco on Saturday nights. Elizabeth could usually talk to either of them about almost anything, yet at this instant, she was too confused to say a word. One part of her wanted to scream and yell and stamp her feet furiously. The other part wanted to disappear quietly and try to pretend that absolutely nothing had happened.

"Liz," George began, "I'm not going to add insult to injury by telling you anything but the real story. It's true: Robin and I—well—we've fallen in love!" For a moment, he cast a tender, wonder-filled gaze in Robin's direction. Then he caught himself and snapped his attention back to Elizabeth. "But you've got to believe me, Liz, as strange as it might sound, we ourselves were kind of hoping it wasn't happening. We kept telling ourselves it was friendship, nothing

109

more. And we fought our real feelings because of Enid, and Allen, too.''

Allen Walters was Robin's long-time boyfriend, a shy, brilliant stringbean of a boy, who'd befriended Robin in the days when she was overweight and nobody else would. And when the gorgeous, slender new Robin had emerged, like a butterfly from a cocoon, and it seemed as if every guy west of the Rockies was trying to get a date with her, she never once went out with anyone but Allen. Until now.

"Eventually, though, we had to own up to what was actually happening,'' George continued.

Elizabeth bit down hard on her trembling lower lip. Perhaps she was supposed to applaud George's honesty, but all she could think about was her best friend. Elizabeth could picture Enid's face perfectly, her green eyes lighting up with pleasure every time she was with George. "How could you do this to Enid?'' Elizabeth blurted out, swallowing against the lump in her throat.

A tear rolled down Robin's cheek, quickly followed by another one. "Oh, Liz, we didn't mean it to happen. Honestly. I mean, Enid's always been so nice to me, and Allen—he's just about the sweetest guy in the world. But—but George and I can't help the way we feel, can we?'' Robin sobbed.

Elizabeth softened at the sight of Robin's fine-featured face, streaked with tears. "I suppose not," she replied, sighing deeply. "And I wish with all my heart that I could be happy for you."

"But you can't be?" George asked, his voice thick with sadness. "Liz, I've always counted you as a friend. Please don't let that change." His gray eyes pleaded with her.

Elizabeth's face was strained with pain and confusion. Where were her allegiances supposed to lie? "Of course you're my friend, George," she said miserably, "but I can't bear the thought of seeing Enid unhappy for even a minute."

"I can't either." George's words were muted, and tears glistened in the corners of his eyes. "That's why it's going to be so hard to tell her."

"But you will do it." Elizabeth was firm. "I mean it wouldn't be fair not to tell her." It was the first thing Elizabeth had felt certain about since she'd pulled the Fiat into the airfield lot.

George nodded. "She's meeting me back out here later tonight. I promised her the first ride up, as soon as I got my license."

"I remember. She's been so excited about that, you know." Elizabeth had shared her friend's enthusiasm all week, but now there was little joy in her voice. If Enid had only known the price she'd pay for that one chance to fly with George.

"I know," George responded with difficulty. "And I won't deny her the pleasure of that ride. But as soon as it's over, I'm going to have to tell her everything." He dabbed at his tears with the edge of his shirt-sleeve.

"And I talked to Allen this morning." Robin sniffled, another stream of tears threatening to break forth.

On the runway nearby, a two-seater plane prepared for takeoff. Elizabeth watched it to avoid having to look at Robin and George. "I guess that's all anyone can expect you to do," she acknowledged, though her words rang with sorrow. It was so unfair—even the best solution would be the cause of so much unhappiness. And there wasn't a thing Elizabeth could do to change that.

After a round of ruefully stilted goodbyes, Elizabeth left the airfield with a hollow feeling in the pit of her stomach. She had accomplished her mission—she'd found out what she'd come to find out—but she felt even worse now than she had on the drive over. Half an hour or so ago, there had been a tiny glimmer of hope. Now there was nothing. Except the hard, cold knowledge that Enid was in for a terrible, heart-wrenching shock. But even Elizabeth had no idea of just how harsh a blow fate was about to deal her very best friend.

Ten

Lila summoned up every ounce of strength she had and tried to lift herself off her canopied bed. But her arms and legs felt weak and rubbery, and her head seemed as if it were filled with cement. She fell back on her pillow almost immediately.

"*Damn!*" she muttered fiercely, the room swimming dizzily around her. "I won't be sick for tonight. I absolutely refuse!" She made one more effort to pull herself out of bed. By sheer, stubborn will alone, she was able to swing her legs around, over the edge of the mattress, so that she was sitting upright.

"Good. One step at a time," she encouraged herself. Gingerly she placed her feet on the floor and hoisted herself into a standing position. Like a calf about to take its first step, she felt her legs threaten to collapse under her. She grabbed onto her night table, steadied herself, and then took several quick steps over toward the full-length mirror on the door to her walk-in closet.

As she caught sight of her reflection, she

uttered a piercing shriek. Her eyes were puffy, bloodshot, and ringed with dark, bluish circles, her nose was red, and her cheeks were drained of any color at all. "Why today?" she yelled, stamping her foot.

The noise brought Eva, the Fowlers' tiny, snowy-haired housekeeper, running up to her room in a panic. "Lila, dear, are you all right?" she cried, as she walked across the room.

"No, I'm not all right," Lila wailed, still staring at herself in the mirror. "In fact, I look like a cross between Dracula and the Wicked Witch of the West. Can't you do something, Eva?"

Eva took one glance at Lila's drawn, wan face. "I certainly can," she answered. "The first thing I can do is put you straight to bed."

"But . . ."

"No buts about it. The second thing I can do is call Dr. Johnstone immediately and have him come right over." Eva folded her arms across her chest.

"No!" Lila shouted out, her eyes filled with dismay. "I just need to put on a little makeup or something. I look worse than I feel." She was instantly sorry that she had let Eva see her.

Eva shook her head. "To bed, Lila. This instant."

Lila knew from years of experience that there was no chance of changing Eva's mind once it was made up. Beneath her frail appearance and sweet voice was the iron determination of a Roman emperor.

Grudgingly Lila allowed Eva to take her by the elbow and help her onto the bed. The truth was that it felt great to lie down again. But Lila wasn't about to admit that to Eva. "Please, Eva," she began pleadingly, "I'll stay here for a little while, but no doctor, OK? I'm sure if I rest I'll feel better in an hour or so."

Eva sighed. "It must be a boy. You had a big date arranged for tonight, isn't that so?"

"Well—yes," Lila confessed. "But you don't really understand, Eva—"

Eva laughed. "Of course I do, dear. I know it's hard to believe, but I was once your age, too."

"Then you'll let me go?" Lila said weakly.

"Sorry," Eva said firmly. "You'll simply have to call him and make it another night. The only man you're going to see tonight is Dr. Johnstone."

Lila groaned. "Don't you feel like an ogre, standing in the path of true love?"

Eva gave a little smile of amusement. "Lila, if he's a nice young man, he'll wait."

That was true, Lila figured. Besides, this was no ordinary guy. This was Jack, her fiancé. What difference could one night possibly make when compared to forever? Jack would certainly understand.

"You win," she told Eva, reaching for the piece of paper on the night table on which Jack

115

had written his address and telephone number. Eva handed her the powder-blue princess phone, and Lila dialed his number. She and Jack were simply going to have to celebrate another evening.

Jessica hung up the telephone in the upstairs hallway, smiling as if she'd just won a million dollars. She immediately raced into Elizabeth's room and plopped down on the bed, where her twin was sitting and looking over one of the first copies of the latest *Oracle*. Jessica's cheeks were flushed with excitement.

Elizabeth looked up. "Let me guess," she teased. "You just finished talking to the Queen of England."

"Better than that!" Jessica replied, her blue-green eyes shining with happiness. "Jack just called me."

"And?" Elizabeth arched one eyebrow questioningly. "Did he break the news about the two of you to Lila?"

"Of course, silly. And we're going out right now to celebrate. Did you ever doubt for a moment that he'd level with her? Wait—no, don't answer that, Liz." A hint of a frown creased Jessica's brow. "But you shouldn't have doubted it." Jessica didn't add that she had begun to feel doubtful herself, when she hadn't heard from Jack on Saturday. But now all doubts had been erased from her mind.

116

The frown changed slowly into a sly grin. "I mean why would any guy want to spend his time with Lila, when he could spend it with me?" She ran her fingers through her hair in an imitation of a femme fatale.

Elizabeth gave her a playful swat on the arm. "Ah, yes, my dear, you are so bee-you-tee-ful, they are breaking down the front door just to get a glimpse of you. In fact, you are almost as bee-you-tee-ful as me." Elizabeth mimicked Jessica's femme fatale imitation perfectly.

"As beautiful as *you*, Liz?" Jessica deadpanned. "Never!" The sisters collapsed on the bed in gales of laughter.

"Well, that's more like it." Jessica giggled and gave Elizabeth a playful swat. "It's no fun to see you moping around here these days, like some prophet of doom. Honestly, you'd think the world was going to collapse under your feet tomorrow, to look at you lately."

Jessica's remarks instantly reminded Elizabeth of what had been bothering her all afternoon. *Not tomorrow*, she thought, *but tonight. And not under my feet but Enid's.* A veil of sorrow clouded her face.

Jessica smacked her forehead with the heel of her hand. "Me and my big mouth!" she said. "Liz, I'm sorry. I didn't mean to get you all bummed out again, but what's the problem now? You're all done with the extra work on *The Oracle*, aren't you?"

117

Elizabeth brightened. "Yeah, I'm bringing an advance copy over to Penny's in a little while, and it looks great, if I do say so myself. Want to see it?" She held the pages out to her twin, hoping to keep the conversation away from her troubles. Even if she *could* tell someone what was bothering her, Jessica was not the logical choice. There wasn't one chance in a billion that she would have any sympathy for Enid.

Elizabeth let out a tiny sigh of relief as her sister took the newspaper and began to look at it. She was off the hook for the moment.

Jessica skimmed the news items carelessly and zeroed right in on "Eyes and Ears," her sister's gossip column. It was Jessica's favorite part of the paper, and she was proud to be able to say that her twin wrote it. "Hmmm," she mused. "Isn't Jamie Duncan that cute new swimmer who just moved here from Florida? Why didn't you tell me about him and Emily Mayer before?"

"You didn't ask," Elizabeth responded lightly. "Besides, now you know."

"How'd that happen so quickly?" Jessica asked.

"It seems Jamie was totally wowed by Emily's drumming at the last Droids concert," Elizabeth told her twin. The Droids were the area's number-one high-school band, and everybody agreed that someday they were destined for stardom. "He went backstage afterward to introduce himself to her, and one thing led to another."

Jessica whistled through her teeth. "He's a fast worker, isn't he?" Then, almost as an afterthought, she shot Elizabeth a curious glance. "You know, Liz, you amaze me sometimes. I mean you never gossip, you don't pay any attention to nasty rumors, but in your own quiet way, you know absolutely everything. How do you manage it?" A hint of admiration tinged Jessica's words.

Elizabeth shrugged modestly. "That's a journalist's job," she replied. "You know—*you've* got to be good at splits and flips and stuff for the cheering squad; I have to know what's going on at school for *The Oracle*."

"That still doesn't explain how you do it," Jessica commented. "But, anyway, soon you'll be able to print a hot new item about your very own sister and her very own, very important new boyfriend." Jessica couldn't possibly have looked more pleased.

Elizabeth gave an exaggerated roll of her eyes. "Oh, yes. The nobleman in disguise." Even though she'd softened toward Jack lately, she still thought all the talk about how he was something akin to royalty had gotten pretty far out of hand.

But Jessica was too busy with thoughts of Jack to catch the note of sarcasm in her sister's voice. She sighed. "Isn't it the most exciting thing?" she said, forgetting altogether about the issue of the newspaper in her hand. "And I bet today's the day I find out exactly who he really is, too. Just imagine it, Liz. The unveiling of my prince!"

Elizabeth gently loosened the copy of *The Oracle* from Jessica's fingers and carefully put it on her own lap. "I suppose he's taking you someplace appropriately regal this afternoon?" she remarked.

"No, that's the great thing about Jack. He's not riding on his family's name or fortune, or anything. Every penny he spends is a penny he earns with his own hands. Just like plain old ordinary people. Isn't that noble?"

"Oh, brother," Elizabeth mumbled under her breath.

But Jessica didn't hear a thing. She was completely absorbed by visions of the afternoon ahead. "So he's taking me to Guido's for a late lunch. Isn't that fantastic?"

Elizabeth had to agree with her twin there. Guido's made the best pizza in all of California— maybe the best anywhere, she thought. "Sounds good, Jess," Elizabeth confirmed. But she had a feeling that she could have told her sister Guido's had burned down earlier in the day and Jessica wouldn't have batted an eyelash.

A happily dazed smile on her lips, Jessica was hopelessly lost in her own private world—a world made for just two people, where Jack was prince and Jessica was his one and only princess.

Eleven

Jessica helped herself to the last piece of the Guido's deluxe pie, smothered in tomato sauce and mozzarella cheese and heaped with six different toppings.

"On a scale of one to ten, how do you think it rates?" Jack asked.

Jessica took a bite out of her slice and chewed it slowly, as if noting every aspect of its rich flavor and texture. "I give it a nine point nine," she finally declared.

"Not a bad score," Jack said, laughing, "but what happened to the other tenth of a point?"

Jessica daintily licked the sauce from her fingers. "Well, nothing's perfect!" she joked. *Except maybe you,* she added silently. Jack looked especially handsome that afternoon, wearing a dark-brown crewneck sweater over a wheat-tone button-down shirt that complemented the color of his hair. Every time Jessica looked at him, tiny ripples of ecstasy washed up and down her spine.

"You know, Jessica," Jack remarked, "I'm not sure I believe it. I think it *is* possible to experience perfection."

"Oh?" Jessica said, leaning forward on her right elbow and gazing up at him. "And do you think you have?"

A faraway look crept into Jack's eyes. "Well, one time my family was down in the Caribbean—I don't know if I told you, but we have a little cottage down there."

"Oh, really?" Jessica could already picture herself stretched out in her sexiest bikini, on a strip of private white sand beach that flanked a spectacular palace—the house that Jack so modestly referred to as the "little cottage." "It must be lovely," she said.

"Yeah, it really is a tropical paradise," Jack confirmed. "Anyway, one day my sister, Valerie, and I decided to go scuba diving off our boat. It was one of those perfect Caribbean days—a light breeze, the sun strong and high in the sky. And the water was a clear, cool, turquoise, kind of like—well, the color of your eyes." Jack paused and flashed Jessica his irresistible smile. Jessica's heart did somersaults that would have made an Olympic gymnast proud.

"It was just one of those days when you know something special is going to happen," Jack continued. "And it did. Valerie and I discovered the most incredible coral reef. There was a whole world down there, unlike anything I had ever seen. Fish as brightly colored as neon lights and all this strange, exotic sea vegetation . . ." Jack's eyes shone brightly. "I know this might sound weird, but we felt like Christopher Columbus discovering America or something, just the two of us, out in the middle of the sea, the sun shimmering way above us on the surface of the water. That was the day I felt as if I knew what perfection was—"

Suddenly Jack was dead silent, leaving his sentence hanging in midair. He was staring at something directly behind Jessica, and he had his face twisted into the strangest grimace. To Jessica it seemed a combination of fear and utter hatred.

Jessica whipped around in her seat to see tall, handsome Nicholas Morrow entering Guido's with a lanky, red-haired boy whom she didn't recognize. They sat down a few tables away, near the artificial waterfall that cascaded down the rear wall of the pizzeria.

"Jack, what's the matter?" Jessica asked with alarm, twisting sideways in her chair so that she could see her date as well as Nicholas and his friend. "Is it something about Nicholas?" She recalled Jack's strange reaction to him at Lila's party.

"No, it's not Nicholas," Jack answered. But Jessica detected the same note of ferocity in his voice that she heard that night at the movies, when she'd asked him about Lila. Jack's eyes were glazed and his knuckles white as he clenched the edge of the table. It seemed almost as if he were locked in some kind of internal struggle.

Over what? Jessica wondered. To gain some kind of control of himself, perhaps?

As had happened that first night, Jessica felt a shudder of fear course through her. But as suddenly as Jack's fierce expression had appeared, it now vanished. His eyes cleared, and his scowl melted. "It's not Nicholas at all," he repeated, this time more convincingly. Jessica felt herself relax a little.

At that moment Nicholas caught sight of them and waved. Jessica waved back, but Jack lowered his head and averted his gaze. "Jessica," he said, the tension creeping back into his voice, "if you're all done, I think I'll go take care of the check. I'll meet you out by the car, OK?"

"OK," Jessica said, puzzlement coloring her face. Something was very wrong. Jack's calm, gentlemanly demeanor was giving way to some most disturbing behavior. It obviously had something to do with Nicholas and his friend, since Jack was doing his best to avoid them.

But why? Jack didn't stick around long enough to answer her question. In the wink of an eye, he had rushed across the large room to the cashier and was now paying for their lunch.

Feeling thoroughly confused, Jessica stood up to follow him out of the restaurant. On the way to the door, she stopped to say a dazed hello to Nicholas and his friend.

Nicholas introduced the red-haired boy. "Jessica Wakefield, this is David Matson. He's visiting me from the East Coast."

"Pleased to meet you," she said, preoccupied. Her eyes were on Jack, who was now heading for the exit.

"David and I graduated from prep school together last year," Nicholas added.

Jessica barely heard him. "That's nice," she murmured, watching Jack disappear through the door. "Look, I don't mean to be rude, but someone's waiting for me outside." She said a hasty goodbye and scrambled out after Jack.

He was leaning against his white Rambler when she caught up to him, looking much more composed than he had a few minutes ago. "I'm awfully sorry about that, Jess," he said immediately, taking her hand. "And I owe you an explanation."

Jessica didn't argue. This whole date seemed to be taking on a decidedly unsavory flavor, and she wasn't pleased about it. If Jack could explain the peculiar turn of events, perhaps they could go back to the idyllic, romantic time they'd been having earlier.

"The truth is," he began, "that I think I've met Nicholas's friend."

"David?" Jessica questioned.

A frown grazed Jack's lips. "Yes, David. That's

his name. I was afraid he might recognize me, and that word would end up getting back to my father. Jessica, I apologize for acting so strangely. I hope you understand." The smile that set Jessica's heart fluttering was back on Jack's face, and his usual charming manner had returned.

Jessica let out a sigh of relief. There *was* a logical reason for Jack's behavior. Thank goodness. Maybe he had overreacted a bit, but so what? He wasn't one-hundred-percent perfect, after all. But he was incredibly handsome. And someone important, as well, she reminded herself. She smiled back at him, a brilliant, dazzling smile. "Apologies accepted," she said, the incident in the pizzeria a thing of the past. "Now you were right in the middle of telling me about the coral reef you discovered." She punctuated her sentence with a tiny kiss on Jack's mouth.

Jack drew her closer and kissed her again, softly, lingeringly. "Yes, the coral reef," he said as their lips parted. "I took some great underwater pictures of it. I have them at my place, if you feel like coming over."

"At your place?" Jessica hesitated only for a second. "Sure, I'd love to come over for a while. I told Liz we might meet her and Todd and a few other people up at Secca Lake later. But I guess we could go to your house for a while first. Sure, why not?" she said, throwing all caution to the wind. Some people might say it wasn't proper to go to the house of a guy you'd known only for a couple of weeks. But she wasn't some people. And Jack was too good-looking to turn down. Besides, there would almost certainly be clues about his background—snapshots of his family or of the mansion, or perhaps a monogram on some sort of personal item. Yes, Jack's house would be the perfect place to discover who he really was.

"What are we waiting for?" Jessica asked as she climbed inside Jack's car.

Nicholas Morrow shook his head as he and David waited to order. "I'm worried about Jessica," he told his friend. "There's something about that guy she was with that makes me kind of nervous."

David ran a hand through his hair. "Nervous?" he asked. "In what way?"

"That's the trouble," Nicholas answered. "I can't really put my finger on it. But the first time I met him, at a party a couple of weeks ago, I thought I knew him from somewhere. When I asked him if I looked familiar, he nearly jumped down my throat, insisting he'd never seen me before. But he took a good hard look at me first.

"Then, a few days later I ran into him at the Sweet Valley Mall. I said hello, but he acted as if he barely knew who I was. I reminded him that we'd been introduced at the party, and he just mumbled something incoherent and staggered away. It was almost as if he was drunk or something. I don't know—he just seems out of whack, somehow."

"I'm sure you know what you're talking about," David affirmed, "but there's not a whole lot of hard-and-fast evidence in what you're saying."

Nicholas chuckled. "That's what I get for being friends with someone who wants to become a lawyer. So you're saying I should just forget the entire thing?"

"Well—no, not exactly. But maybe you should take a closer look at the facts. Where do you think you know this guy from, anyway?"

"I'm not sure," Nicholas replied, "but he looks a little like someone I used to see on campus the first few weeks I was at prep school. You didn't recognize him, did you?"

"I only looked at him for a second," David said, "when you waved to them. And he had his head down. But come to think of it, he did seem sort of familiar."

"Ah-ha!" Nicholas shouted triumphantly. "Then I must have been right. He did go to school with us!"

"Maybe so," David agreed. "But I can't quite place his face." He furrowed his brow, trying to figure out where he had seen Jessica's date before.

"I wonder why Jack made such a point of

insisting that he didn't know me?" Nicholas mused.

Suddenly David's freckled face went as white as a nurse's uniform. "Nicholas," he croaked, "what did you say his name was?"

Nicholas noted the look of alarm in his friend's eyes. "It's Jack," he replied, worried. "I don't know his last name."

"You were right," David said, his voice a frightened whisper. "He did go to school with us—before he got kicked out. And your friend—Jessica—may be in big trouble."

"What do you mean?" Nicholas's tone now matched David's.

"Something happened when you first transferred from your other school," David said, "and were just getting settled, so maybe you didn't hear much about it. But a student, Jack—yes, I'm almost positive he's the same one—robbed a girl at knifepoint, a girl he'd been dating, in fact."

"Oh, my god!" gasped Nicholas. "It can't be true. I mean I thought he was bad news, but I never dreamed . . ." His sentence trailed off as the full impact of David's disclosure hit him.

"It's true," David said. "The girl never filed charges, but he was expelled from school immediately."

Nicholas jumped up and grabbed his friend by the arm. "Dave, we've got to find Jessica and warn her!"

The two boys raced out to Nicholas's Jeep, and in no time flat they were peeling out of the restaurant parking lot. "The Wakefields'—we've got to get to the Wakefields'," Nicholas said as he sped in the direction of their split-level house in the valley. "Maybe someone over there knows where Jessica and Jack were headed next."

The Jeep careened around a bend, tires squealing. "David, do you think the same thing could happen again?" Nicholas asked. Panic laced his words.

"I don't know, Nicholas." David's voice, too, teetered on the brink of control. "A lot of strange stories started going around about him after that incident at school."

"Such as?" Nicholas stepped down harder on the gas pedal.

"Well, from what I can piece together, he was something of a modern-day Dr. Jekyll and Mr. Hyde. Most of the time he was a great guy— nice, polite, the kind of person everybody gets along with. But every so often, he'd just go wild and lose control of himself."

"Why?" Nicholas wanted to know.

"It's a sad story," David began. "It seems Jack's entire family was killed in a boating accident a few years before he came to school. There was a sister, a younger sister, I think, whom he was particularly close to. Anyway, rumor has it that from the day they died, Jack started escaping into his own little fantasy world, where his sister was still alive and where Jack could be anything he wanted to be.

"The whole situation got worse when his uncle, whom he'd been living with since the accident, scraped up enough money to send him away to school. This was about a year and a half before you arrived," David explained.

"Anyway, you know how many wealthy kids there were up at school?" David continued. It was more a statement than a question, Nicholas himself coming from a well-to-do family. "Well, it seems that in Jack's fantasy world he saw himself as even richer and more important than they were. He started telling people stories about himself. Pretty soon, I'm not sure even he knew what was real and what wasn't."

"Wow, that's pretty heavy stuff," Nicholas murmured, as he turned the Jeep onto Calico Drive.

"That's not the worst of it," David related somberly. "I guess that double life grew pretty hard to handle. So he started getting into drugs. That only made his problems harder to control."

"That'd explain why he was so out of it at the mall," Nicholas observed, shaking his head. "So what else happened?"

"Apparently he started stealing to keep himself supplied with drugs and with possessions to fit the new social position he'd dreamed up. For instance, he was always perfectly dressed."

"Yes, that's still true." Nicholas pulled into the

Wakefields' driveway, and he and David jumped out of the Jeep.

"The amazing thing," David concluded as they hurried up the front walk, "is that drugs and all, he got away with it for so long. One thing's for sure—the guy's a first-rate actor. From what the girl up at school told her friends, he never let his disguise down for a moment. Until the day she started asking too many personal questions and he felt as though he were being trapped in his own lies. Then—well, then the Mr. Hyde in him took over, and he turned into a very dangerous character. . . ."

As Nicholas rang the Wakefields' doorbell, his face was set in a grim expression. "Well, let's just pray that we find Jessica before that happens to her."

Elizabeth closed the Ayalas' door behind her, a happy smile on her face. Everything had worked out beautifully between Penny and Tina. Penny was so proud of her little sister that she'd made her a staff photographer for *The Oracle* right then and there.

Tina, for her part, had thrown her arms around Penny and admitted that she had the perfect big sister after all, and that she'd just been too stubborn to realize it.

Now, as Elizabeth crossed the Ayalas' front lawn and climbed into the Fiat, she felt very good about the way things had worked out between Penny and Tina. It helped to lift her out of her bleak mood over Enid and George.

She started up the little red convertible and began backing down the Ayalas' driveway. Suddenly a Jeep came whipping around the corner and screeched to a stop at the bottom of the driveway, blocking the Fiat's path. Elizabeth turned her head around to see what was going on.

"Liz, thank goodness we found you!" Nicholas Morrow raced from his car to Elizabeth's, David following close behind. "Your father told us you might be stopping here on your way up to Secca Lake."

Elizabeth took one look at the troubled expression in Nicholas's green eyes, and her heart plummeted. "Nicholas—what's wrong? What's happened?"

Nicholas quickly explained, and the color drained from Elizabeth's cheeks. "My god, Nicholas! Jessica's with Jack right this second!"

"We know," put in David. "We just saw them leave Guido's. We thought you might know where they were going next."

Elizabeth shook her head. "They could be anywhere. And if I know my sister, she's probably grilling him about his background right now." Elizabeth could hear Jessica's voice in her ears: "I bet today's the day I find out exactly who Jack really is."

"And if Jessica pushes too hard for answers,"

Nicholas said gravely, "she's going to end up in great danger!"

"Todd and the people up at the lake are just going to have to wait. Oh, Nicholas, we don't have a minute to lose!" Elizabeth's voice was laced with panic. "But I don't have any idea where to start searching for her!"

Twelve

Jessica looked around the small, shabbily furnished room that Jack called home.

"It might not look like much," Jack said, as if reading her mind, "but I did it all without my father's help or money."

"So I see," Jessica observed, trying to keep the note of disappointment out of her voice. She'd expected at least some small indication, some memento of his past life. But there was nothing except a threadbare rug over a dull linoleum floor, a battered chest of drawers, a tiny table with two metal-frame chairs, and an ancient fold-out couch. Jessica seated herself tensely on the edge of one of the chairs. She'd never been in an apartment quite this gloomy before.

Jack settled down on the couch and surveyed Jessica intently. "What's the matter?" he asked. "You did want to see where I lived, didn't you?"

Jessica nodded. "I guess it just wasn't what I expected."

"Oh?" Jack asked. For the merest fraction of a

135

second, Jessica thought she saw the glazed expression in his eyes that she'd noticed at Guido's. But it was gone before she had a chance to be sure.

"You know you can get awfully tired of posh, when you've been surrounded by it your whole life," Jack explained.

"You can?" Jessica said in a small voice.

"Yup. But you didn't come here to talk about that," Jack said, yet again avoiding the subject of his background. "You came to see my underwater pictures." He opened the door to his one closet and began hunting around for his photographs.

Jessica tried to peer around him, to see if there were any momentos hidden in the closet, but there were so many things crammed inside that it was impossible to tell.

"Ah-ha! Here we go!" Jack pulled a big scrapbook from the top closet shelf. As he did, a picture fluttered to the ground.

Jessica went over and picked it up. On it was a little blond girl of about eleven or twelve, with Jack's smile and his deep-set eyes. "Oh, is this your sister?" Jessica asked. The girl stood in front of a very ordinary, yellow, two-story house.

Jack dropped the scrapbook on the table and nearly grabbed the photo out of Jessica's hand. "Yes, that's Valerie," he said, his voice strained.

Jessica shot him a quizzical look. For a considerate person, he'd certainly had his share of inconsiderate moments that day. She tried to think of something to say to ease the tension. "She's very pretty," Jessica offered tentatively.

"Yes . . ." A peculiar forlornness echoed in that one syllable.

"Do you have any more recent pictures of her?" Jessica asked.

"No!" Jack roared.

Then Jessica saw it. The glazed expression was back again. "Look," she said anxiously, "maybe I'd better go."

Jack sank down on the couch and took a few deep breaths. "Don't," he said. "I really want you to see those scuba-diving pictures. Please stay," he added simply. The old Jack was back again, the one who'd named the star after Jessica.

But Jessica was on her guard now. She didn't know how many more of these strange, tense moments she could handle. "I don't know, Jack—" she began.

Jack held his hand out to her. "Jessica, I want to be with you." Jack flashed her his irresistible smile. "Please."

"Well—OK," Jessica conceded finally. After all, she'd worked hard for this moment—just Jack and her, Lila no more than a shadow in the past. She didn't want to blow it now.

When she began looking at the photographs, Jessica was glad she'd stayed. They were truly beautiful, and after seeing them, she felt very close to Jack.

But there was still one big disappointment to her afternoon. Jack seemed to have no intention at all of unveiling himself to her. And Jessica suspected that if she didn't take matters into her own hands, she'd leave knowing no more about him than she did right now.

"Jack," she said, a plan taking shape in her mind, "can I use the bathroom?"

"Right over there," Jack pointed.

"Don't go anywhere," Jessica joked, giving him a wink. She went into the bathroom and shut the door behind her. Then, as quickly and quietly as she could, she began opening all the bathroom cabinets, hunting on the floor, searching every nook and cranny. There had to be some telltale item—a shaving kit with Jack's initials stamped in gold, or a prescription bottle with his full name on it. Jessica opened zippered cases, poked behind every tube and jar, and even checked the shower stall.

Finally, in the little cabinet under the sink, she found an unmarked rectangular box. Eagerly she pried the lid open. What she saw inside made her gasp. Drugs. All kinds of drugs. And not the prescription kind she was hoping to find. There were pills of all different colors and sizes, a jar of whitish powder, a plastic bag full of marijuana, pipes, rolling papers, and various other accessories that Jessica couldn't even begin to identify.

But she knew trouble when she saw it. This had to be the reason for Jack's strange behavior. And so much for his excuse about the chlorine in the community center pool. Jack's glazed, red eyes and his disturbing flare-ups suddenly made sense to Jessica. It was painfully clear that Jack was in no way the boy she thought he was. Suddenly Jessica was very angry at Jack, and she raced from the bathroom to confront him.

"Why didn't you tell me about this?" she cried, still holding the box. She burst into the cramped living area just in time to see Jack pull his hand out of her shoulder bag, guilt written all over his face.

"Oh, my god," she yelled. "Now what's happening. What are you doing in my bag?"

"Shh, Jessica, I can explain," Jack answered her. "I was looking for a match. You have to light my stove with a match." He gestured toward the tiny two-burner stove in the corner of the room. "I was going to make us some tea."

But Jessica had heard enough of his explanations. It was as if a light had just gone on in her head. "Well, what about this? Can you explain this?" She shook the box in her hand.

Jack seemed to notice it for the first time, and he grew deathly pale.

"And what about the money that disappeared the night we went to the movies? Can you explain that? And Lila's father's cuff links, what about those?'' Pieces of the puzzle were falling into place with alarming speed.

"Jessica—don't. Don't say another word.'' Suddenly Jack's tone became menacing.

"Why? Don't you like hearing the truth about yourself, you—you phony?'' Jessica spluttered angrily.

Jack was on Jessica in a second. She struggled with every muscle in her body to break free of his grasp, but he was too strong.

"I'm sorry! I didn't mean it! I take it back!'' Tears of fright streamed down her cheeks. But something inside Jack had snapped. He was relentless. Jessica felt her cries choked off as Jack pinned her to the ground and closed his hands around her throat!

Elizabeth dialed Lila Fowler's telephone number, her fingers trembling. This was her last chance to locate Jessica. They'd been up to Miller's Point, through town, and finally out to the mall. There had been no sign of Jack's Rambler anywhere. Now, as she stood at a pay phone by the Valley Cinema, Elizabeth held her breath and prayed.

On the third ring, Lila picked up the phone. "Hello?'' she croaked weakly.

"Lila? It's Liz Wakefield. Are you OK?''

"Oh, hi, Liz. No, I have the twenty-four hour flu, as a matter of fact,'' Lila said self-pityingly. "The doctor was just here.''

"Oh, I'm really sorry to hear that," Elizabeth responded. "And I'm sorry to bother you, but I'm afraid I've got an emergency on my hands. I need Jack's address immediately." Urgency echoed in her voice.

Suddenly Lila's voice rose to a shrill, hysterical pitch. "Jack? What's happened to Jack? Is he all right?"

"Jack's fine, Lila," Elizabeth informed her, in words tinged with anxiety. "But Jessica might not be. That's who I'm looking for."

"Oh." Lila spoke quietly again. "But what would Jessica be doing at Jack's?" she asked innocently.

Elizabeth took a deep breath. This was going to be more difficult than she had realized. "She's been seeing him," Elizabeth finally said, opting for the simple, unadorned truth. There was just no time for diplomacy.

There was silence on the other end of the line. "Lila? Lila, are you there?" Elizabeth asked. She had to get that address as quickly as possible.

"The traitor!" Lila shrieked. "How could she?" Elizabeth held the receiver away from her ear, but she could still hear Lila's screams. "I'm going to kill her. I swear it!"

Elizabeth didn't have time to wait for Lila's tirade to wind down. Every second was a second wasted. "Lila," she yelled into the phone, "listen to me. You don't want him anyway."

"What do you mean I don't want him?" Lila

yelled, without giving Elizabeth a chance to explain. "You don't know a thing about our relationship, anyway."

"But I know something about Jack that you don't know. Lila, he's nothing more than a common crook. And a dangerous one at that."

"What?" Lila's horrified cry rang out across the phone lines.

"I'm sorry, Lila. I know how much it must hurt." Elizabeth wished she didn't have to be the one to break the news. But there was no time to worry about that now. Not with Jessica's safety at stake. She went on to give Lila a quick version of Jack's history.

When Lila spoke again, her voice was low and calm. But it was like the lull before a raging storm. "Elizabeth, Jack lives at Thirty-eight Vine Street, near the railroad tracks."

"Thank you, Lila. You don't know how much your help means." Elizabeth hoped she could get off the phone before Lila unleashed her fury once again.

"Oh, and Liz? When you find Jessica, tell her she did me a huge favor!" Elizabeth jumped as Lila slammed down the receiver. She knew that in the Fowler mansion, the storm had broken out. But Elizabeth had gotten what she so vitally needed—Jack's address.

"Follow me," she shouted to Nicholas and David, as she hopped back into the Fiat.

Elizabeth screeched around turns and flew

down the streets of Sweet Valley as if she were a racer in the Indianapolis 500. In almost no time she'd crossed the railroad tracks, steered onto Vine Street, and come to an abrupt halt in front of number thirty-eight. She, Nicholas, and David raced through the door.

But once inside, they were faced with yet another hurdle. There were eight mailboxes in the entryway. That meant eight different apartments. Which one was Jack's?

Elizabeth scanned the mailboxes for names, but many of them were marked with last names only, and some had no names at all.

"Bart Parnello," Elizabeth read out loud. "Apartment two B. I guess we can eliminate that one. And K. Spencer, three A. That one, too. But there are still six more apartments." Panic closed in on her. "What should we do?"

"I don't see that we have any choice but to start knocking on doors," Nicholas observed darkly.

The threesome went farther inside the old, dark building and rang the buzzer of the first apartment they came to. No answer. They rang again. Just as they were about to go on to the next door, they heard faint footsteps inside. The door was edged open a crack, and a heavyset man in an undershirt and boxer shorts peered out at them.

"Whadya want?" he snarled. "I'm right in the middle of watching TV."

"We're awfully sorry, sir," Elizabeth said, "but we're looking for someone who lives in this building—a boy named Jack."

"Don't know him!" snapped the man, starting to close the door.

With lightning reflexes, Elizabeth stuck her foot out so her toes were inside the door frame. "Please," she begged, "you have to help us."

"Look," the man bellowed. "Nobody invited you in. So get lost. Understand?"

"I understand that you're the rudest, meanest man I've ever met!" Elizabeth screamed back. Tears of frustration streamed down her face. They were losing precious seconds. In a move of sheer desperation, Elizabeth threw herself against the door, forcing it to open wider, and took another step inside. "Look, I really am sorry I interrupted you, but we need help. And you're not getting rid of me until we get it," she cried.

"Listen, I could pick you up and throw you right out," the man said.

"The boy we're looking for is tall, light-brown hair, about eighteen," Elizabeth plunged ahead boldly.

"If I told you it sounded like the guy in four B, would you leave me alone?" the man growled.

His question needed no answer. Elizabeth, Nicholas, and David were already sprinting up the stairs, toward the building's top floor.

"What are you going to do with me?" Jessica

sobbed. Jack had eased his fingers from around her throat, but he still had her pinned to the floor, his knee digging into her ribcage.

"Oh, Jessica," Jack said in an alarmingly quiet tone, "if only you hadn't been so curious. I really liked you."

"Well, if you like me, you'll let me go, right?" Jessica's teeth chattered with terror as she spoke.

"I said *liked*, Jessica. That wasn't very nice of you to snoop through my things like that."

"I'm sorry. I swear I am!" Jessica was at Jack's mercy. "Please, please, let me up."

"I'm sorry, Jessica, but the party's over. If I let you leave, you'll tell everyone exactly what happened."

"No, I promise I won't. Just let me go home, and I won't say a word."

"Jessica, I'm tired of running from one place to another. I've got a good thing going here in Sweet Valley, and I'm not going to let anyone mess it up for me."

"I won't. Please, Jack, don't hurt me." Jessica was consumed with fear.

"I can't take any chances, Jessica. I have to make sure you won't talk."

Suddenly a cry split the air, accompanied by banging on Jack's door. "Jess! Jessica, are you in there?"

"Liz!" Jessica screamed. "Liz, help me!" Out of the corner of her eye, she could see the doorknob twisting and the door shake, but the single bolt held fast.

"Liz, it's locked!" she screamed, dread rising in her throat.

"Don't worry, Jessica," came Nicholas Morrow's rich baritone. Never before had his voice been so welcome a sound. "We'll get you out if we have to break this door down." He and David began pounding and kicking to loosen the bolt.

Jessica held her breath as the old, poorly fastened lock began to give way.

But Jack had one eye on the door also. "Stop!" he commanded. "Or I'll have to hurt Jessica." His voice rang out through the thin door into the hallway. Instantly the banging ceased.

"No, keep at it!" Jessica yelled. "You're almost there!" The noise started up again immediately.

"You're going to be sorry you said that." Jack's eyes blazed with fury as he yanked Jessica off the floor and dragged her to the tiny kitchen area at the far corner of the apartment. Gripping her with only one hand now, he stretched the other one toward a plastic bin that held his kitchen utensils and clasped the handle of a large knife.

Jessica let out a bloodcurdling scream.

"Quiet!" Jack ordered, raising the knife toward her neck.

But at that instant, the bolt finally gave way, and Nicholas flew into the room, Elizabeth and David close on his heels. Before Jessica could ven blink, Nicholas was fighting to wrest the knife from Jack's powerful grasp. In the struggle, essica broke free, but Jack and Nicholas emained locked in combat. As they wrestled down to the ground, David jumped in to aid his friend, trying to pry the knife from Jack's fingers. But Jack had the maniacal strength of several men. He made wild slashing motions with his arm, catching Nicholas's shoulder with the tip of his knife. Nicholas's shirt was cut open, and a nasty red gash stained the white fabric.

Spurred to action, Jessica forced herself to move back toward Jack. Taking careful aim, she et loose her strongest, best cheerleading kick, catching Jack in the arm. The knife flew out of his hand and landed several feet away on the tattered rug.

After that, it was over in a few short seconds. Elizabeth rushed forward and grabbed the knife, Nicholas struck Jack a driving punch in the stomach with his good arm, and while Jack was doubled over, David grabbed his arms and pinned them behind his back.

Jessica was safe. And the game was finally up for Sweet Valley's mystery prince.

Thirteen

Jessica stood in the Sweet Valley police station a little while later, as the officer on desk duty finished typing up the statement she had made concerning the events of the past few hours. With her were Elizabeth and her parents; David and Nicholas, his left shoulder now bandaged though not too badly hurt.

Behind the front desk, the police radio crackled as policemen called in reports from their assigned locations.

"I hope they lock Jack up and throw away the key," Jessica said ferociously, signing the statement the officer placed in front of her.

Dark-haired, athletic Ned Wakefield put an arm around his daughter's shoulder. "Jess, sweetheart, I know this has been a terrifying ordeal, and it's only natural to feel like you want to get even with Jack, but frankly, I think professional counseling might do a lot more for a troubled boy like that than putting him behind bars could."

"Your father's right," Alice Wakefield put in. "There are special places where they can treat people like Jack. Maybe if he'd gotten help sooner, this whole thing wouldn't have happened."

"And if I hadn't been so dense about going to see his dumb underwater photos, it wouldn't have happened either," Jessica berated herself.

"Jessica, those pictures weren't even Jack's," Elizabeth informed her twin. "David says the girl at school was an expert diver, and they probably belonged to her." David nodded in confirmation.

"More lies. I should have known. I should have sensed it. But no. I was too busy congratulating myself on my new, very important boyfriend. Stupid, stupid me." Jessica hung her head in shame.

"It's not your fault, Jess. He's a very clever, expert liar," Elizabeth said. "There's no question about that. Anyone would have been fooled."

"Liz, I appreciate your trying to make me feel better," Jessica said to her twin, "but *you* weren't fooled. You knew there was something strange about him. No, it was just me who was so blind."

"You shouldn't blame yourself, Jessica." This time Nicholas attempted to console her. "In fact, you ought to feel awfully pleased with yourself. After all, you were the one who got the knife

149

away from Jack. If it weren't for you, who know what might have happened?"

"You're the heroine of the day!" Elizabeth added.

A tiny smile finally appeared on Jessica's lips "I am?"

"Of course you are, silly," her twin replied.

The smile broadened. "And does the heroine get a special dinner out tonight in her honor?" she asked.

"That's my Jessica." Ned Wakefield laughed.

"Does that mean yes?"

"Jess, if you're feeling up to it, you name the place, and we'll go there later!"

Before Jessica had a chance to reply, however, everyone's attention was caught by the police radio, blasting an urgent message through the station. "Small aircraft in trouble. Vicinity of Secca Lake. I repeat, small plane in trouble. Craft number BA three-two-nine. Rented to one George Warren."

Elizabeth let out a horrified gasp. George and Enid! The ordeal was not over yet!

Can George and Enid avert disaster? Find out in Sweet Valley High #20, **CRASH LANDING!**

A LETTER TO THE READER

Dear Friend,

Ever since I created the series, SWEET VALLEY HIGH, I've been thinking about a love trilogy, a miniseries revolving around one very special girl, a character similar in some ways to Jessica Wakefield, but even more devastating—more beautiful, more charming, and much more devious.

Her name is Caitlin Ryan, and with her long black hair, her magnificent blue eyes and ivory complexion, she's the most popular girl at the exclusive boarding school she attends in Virginia. On the surface her life seems perfect. She has it all: great wealth, talent, intelligence, and the dazzle to charm every boy in the school. But deep inside there's a secret need that haunts her life.

Caitlin's mother died in childbirth, and her father abandoned her immediately after she was born. At least that's the lie she has been told by her enormously rich grandmother, the cold and powerful matriarch who has raised Caitlin and given her everything money can buy. But not love.

Caitlin dances from boy to boy, never staying long, often breaking hearts, yet she's so sparkling and delightful that everyone forgives her. No one can resist her.

No one that is, but Jed Michaels. He's the new boy in school—tall, wonderfully handsome, and very, very nice. And Caitlin means to have him.

But somehow the old tricks don't work; she can't

seem to manipulate him. Impossible! There has never been anyone that the beautiful and terrible Caitlin couldn't have. And now she wants Jed Michaels—no matter who gets hurt or what she has to do to get him.

So many of you follow my SWEET VALLEY HIGH series that I know you'll find it fascinating to read what happens when love comes into the life of this spoiled and selfish beauty—the indomitable Caitlin Ryan.

Thanks for being there, and keep reading,

Francine Pascal

A special preview of the exciting
opening chapter of the first book
in the fabulous new trilogy:

CAITLIN

BOOK ONE

LOVING

---

by Francine Pascal,
creator of the best-selling
SWEET VALLEY HIGH series

"That's not a bad idea, Tenny," Caitlin said as she reached for a book from her locker. "Actually, it's pretty good."

"You really like it?" Tenny Sears hung on every word the beautiful Caitlin Ryan said. It was the petite freshman's dream to be accepted into the elite group the tall, dark-haired junior led at Highgate Academy. She was ready to do anything to belong.

Caitlin looked around and noticed the group of five girls who had begun to walk their way, and she lowered her voice conspiratorially. "Let me think it over, and I'll get back to you later. Meanwhile let's just keep it between us, okay?"

"Absolutely." Tenny struggled to keep her excitement down to a whisper. The most important girl in the whole school liked her idea. "Cross my heart," she promised. "I won't breathe a word to anyone."

Tenny would have loved to continue the conversation, but at just that moment Caitlin remembered she'd left her gold pen in French class. Tenny was only too happy to race to fetch it.

The minute the younger girl was out of sight, Caitlin gathered the other girls around her.

"Hey, you guys, I just had a great idea for this year's benefit night. Want to hear it?"

Of course they wanted to hear what she had to say about the benefit, the profits of which would go to the scholarship fund for miners' children. Everyone was always interested in anything Caitlin Ryan had to say. She waited until all eyes were on her, then hesitated for an instant, increasing the dramatic impact of her words.

"How about a male beauty contest?"

"A what?" Morgan Conway exclaimed.

"A male beauty contest," Caitlin answered, completely unruffled. "With all the guys dressing up in crazy outfits. It'd be a sellout!"

Most of the girls looked at Caitlin as if she'd suddenly gone crazy, but Dorothy Raite, a sleek, blond newcomer to Highgate, stepped closer to Caitlin's locker. "I think it's a great idea!"

"Thanks, Dorothy," Caitlin said, smiling modestly.

"I don't know." Morgan was doubtful. "How are you going to get the guys to go along with this? I can't quite picture Roger Wake parading around on stage in a swimsuit."

"He'll be the first contestant to sign up when I get done talking to him." Caitlin's tone was slyly smug.

"And all the other guys?"

"They'll follow along." Caitlin placed the last of her books in her knapsack, zipped it shut, then gracefully slung it over her shoulder. "Everybody who's anybody in this school will just shrivel up and die if they can't be part of it. Believe me, I wouldn't let the student council down. After all, I've got my new presidency to live up to."

Morgan frowned. "I suppose." She took a chocolate bar out of her brown leather shoulder bag and began to unwrap it.

Just at that moment, Tenny came back, empty-handed and full of apologies. "Sorry, Caitlin, I asked all over, but nobody's seen it."

"That's okay. I think I left it in my room, anyway."

"Did you lose something?" Kim Verdi asked, but Caitlin dismissed the subject, saying it wasn't important.

For an instant Tenny was confused until Dorothy Raite asked her if she'd heard Caitlin's fabulous new idea for a male beauty contest. Then everything fell into place. Caitlin had sent her away in order to take credit for the idea.

It didn't even take three seconds for Tenny to make up her mind about what to do. "Sounds terrific," she said. Tenny Sears was determined to belong to this group, no matter what.

Dorothy leaned over and whispered to Caitlin. "Speaking of beauties, look who's walking over here."

Casually Caitlin glanced up at the approaching Highgate soccer star. Roger Wake's handsome face broke into a smile when he saw her. Caitlin knew he was interested in her, and up until then she'd offhandedly played with that interest—when she was in the mood.

"And look who's with him!" Dorothy's elbow nearly poked a hole in Caitlin's ribs. "Jed Michaels. Oh, my God, I've been absolutely dying to meet this guy."

Caitlin nodded, her eyes narrowing. She'd been anxious to meet Jed, too, but she didn't tell Dorothy that. Ever since his arrival as a transfer student at Highgate, Caitlin had been studying him, waiting for precisely the right moment to be introduced and to make an unforgettable impression on him. It seemed that the opportunity had just been handed to her.

"Hey, Caitlin. How're you doing?" Roger called out, completely ignoring the other girls in the group.

"Great, Roger. How about you?" Caitlin's smile couldn't have been wider. "Thought you'd be on the soccer field by now."

"I'm on my way. The coach pushed back practice half an hour today, anyway. Speaking of which, I don't remember seeing you at the last scrimmage." There was a hint of teasing in his voice.

Caitlin looked puzzled and touched her fingertips to her lips. "I was there, I'm sure—"

"We were late, Caitlin, remember?" Tenny spoke up eagerly. "I was with you at drama club, and it ran over."

"Now, how could I have forgotten? You see,

Roger"—Caitlin sent him a sly, laughing look—"we never let the team down. Jenny should know—she's one of your biggest fans."

"Tenny," the girl corrected meekly. But she was glowing from having been singled out for attention by Caitlin.

"Oh, right, Tenny. Sorry, but I'm really bad with names sometimes." Caitlin smiled at the girl with seeming sincerity, but her attention returned quickly to the two boys standing nearby.

"Caitlin," Dorothy burst in, "do you want to tell him—"

"Shhh," Caitlin put her finger to her lips. "Not yet. We haven't made all our plans."

"Tell me what?" Roger asked eagerly.

"Oh, just a little idea we have for the council fund-raiser, but it's too soon to talk about it."

"Come on." Roger was becoming intrigued. "You're not being fair, Caitlin."

She paused. "Well, since you're our star soccer player, I can tell you it's going to be the hottest happening at Highgate this fall."

"Oh, yeah? What, a party?"

"No."

"A concert?"

She shook her head, her black-lashed, blue eyes twinkling. "I'm not going to stand here and play Twenty Questions with you, Roger. But when we decide to make our plans public, you'll be the first to know. I promise."

"Guess I'll have to settle for that."

"Anyway, Roger, I promise not to let any of this other stuff interfere with my supporting the team from now on."

At her look, Roger seemed ready to melt into his Nikes.

Just at that moment Jed Michaels stepped forward. It was a casual move on his part, as though he were just leaning in a little more closely to hear the conversation. His gaze rested on Caitlin.

Although she'd deliberately given the impression of being impervious to Jed, Caitlin was acutely aware of every move he made. She'd studied him enough from a distance to know that she liked what she saw.

Six feet tall, with broad shoulders and a trim body used to exercise, Jed Michaels was the type of boy made for a girl like Caitlin. He had wavy, light brown hair, ruggedly even features, and an endearing, crooked smile. Dressed casually in a striped cotton shirt, tight cords, and western boots, Jed didn't look like the typical preppy Highgate student, and Caitlin had the feeling it was a deliberate choice. He looked like his own person.

Caitlin had been impressed before, but now that she saw him close at hand, she felt electrified. For that brief instant when his incredible green eyes had looked directly into hers, she'd felt a tingle go up her spine.

Suddenly realizing the need for an introduction, Roger put his hand on Jed's shoulder. "By the way, do you girls know Jed Michaels? He just transferred here from Montana. We've already got him signed up for the soccer team."

Immediately the girls called out a chorus of enthusiastic greetings, which Jed acknowledged with a friendly smile and a nod of his head. "Nice to meet you." Dorothy's call had been the loudest, and Jed's gaze went toward the pretty blonde.

Dorothy smiled at him warmly, and Jed grinned back. But before another word could be spoken, Caitlin riveted Jed with her most magnetic look.

"I've seen you in the halls, Jed, and hoped you'd been made welcome." The intense fire of her deep blue eyes emphasized her words.

He looked from Dorothy to Caitlin. "Sure have."

"And how do you like Highgate?" Caitlin pressed on quickly, keeping the attention on herself.

"So far, so good." His voice was deep and soft and just slightly tinged with a western drawl.

"I'm glad." The enticing smile never left Caitlin's lips. "What school did you transfer from?"

"A small one back in Montana. You wouldn't have heard of it."

"Way out in cattle country?"

His eyes glimmered. "You've been to Montana?"

"Once. Years ago with my grandmother. It's really beautiful. All those mountains . . ."

"Yeah. Our ranch borders the Rockies."

"Ranch, huh? I'll bet you ride, then."

"Before I could walk."

"Then you'll have to try the riding here—eastern style. It's really fantastic! We're known for our hunt country in this part of Virginia."

"I'd like to try it."

"Come out with me sometime, and I'll show you the trails. I ride almost every afternoon." Caitlin drew her fingers through her long, black hair, pulling it away from her face in a way she knew was becoming, yet which seemed terribly innocent.

"Sounds like something I'd enjoy,"—Jed said, smiling—"once I get settled in."

"We're not going to give him much time for riding," Roger interrupted. "Not until after soccer season, anyway. The coach already has him singled out as first-string forward."

"We're glad you're on the team," Caitlin said. "With Roger as captain, we're going to have a great season." Caitlin glanced at Roger, who seemed flattered by her praise. Then through slightly lowered lashes, she looked directly back at Jed. "But I know it will be even better now."

Jed only smiled. "Hope I can live up to that."

Roger turned to Jed. "We've got to go."

"Fine." Jed nodded.

Caitlin noticed Dorothy, who had been silent during Jed and Caitlin's conversation. She was now staring at Jed wistfully as he and Roger headed toward the door.

Caitlin quickly leaned over to whisper, "Dorothy, did you notice the way Roger was looking at you?"

Her attention instantly diverted, Dorothy looked away from Jed to look at Caitlin. "Me?" She sounded surprised.

"Yeah. He really seems interested."

"Oh, I don't think so." Despite her attraction to Jed, Dorothy seemed flattered. "He's hardly ever looked at me before."

"You were standing behind me and probably couldn't notice, but take my word for it."

Dorothy glanced at the star soccer player's retreating back. Her expression was doubtful, but for the moment she'd forgotten her pursuit of Jed, and Caitlin took that opportunity to focus her own attention on the new boy from Montana. She knew she only had a moment more to make that unforgettable impression on him before the two boys were gone. Quickly she walked forward. Her voice was light but loud enough to carry to the girls behind her.

"We were just going in your direction, anyway," she called. "Why don't we walk along just to show you what strong supporters of the team we are?"

Looking surprised, Roger said, "That's fine by us. Right, Jed?"

"Whatever you say."

Caitlin thought he sounded pleased by the attention. Quickly, before the other girls joined them, she stepped between the two boys. Roger immediately tried to pull her hand close to his side. She wanted to swat him off, but instead, gave his hand a squeeze, then let go. She was pleased when Diana fell in step beside Roger. Turning to Jed, Caitlin smiled and said, "There must be a thousand questions you still have about the school and the area. Have you been to Virginia before?"

"A few times. I've seen a little of the countryside."

"And you like it?"

As they walked out the door of the building, Jed turned his head so that he could look down into her upturned face and nodded. There was a bright twinkle in his eyes.

Caitlin took that twinkle as encouragement, and her own eyes grew brighter. "So much goes on around here at this time of year. Has anyone told you about the fall dance this weekend?"

"I think Matt Jenks did. I'm rooming with him."

"It'll be great—a real good band," Caitlin cooed. In the background she heard the sound of the others' voices, but they didn't matter. Jed Michaels was listening to *her*.

They walked together for only another minute, down the brick footpath that connected the classroom buildings to the rest of the elegant campus. Caitlin told him all she could about the upcoming dance, stopping short of asking him to be her date. She wasn't going to throw herself at him. She wouldn't have to, anyway. She knew it would be only a matter of time before he would be hers.

It didn't take them long to reach the turnoff for the soccer field. "I guess this is where I get off," she said lightly. "See you around."

"See you soon," he answered and left.

Caitlin smiled to herself. This handsome boy from Montana wasn't going to be an easy mark, but this was an adequate beginning. She wanted him—and what Caitlin wanted, Caitlin got.

"You going back to the dorm, Caitlin?" Morgan asked.

"Yeah, I've got a ton of reading to do for English lit." Caitlin spoke easily, but her thoughts were on the smile Jed Michaels had given her just before he'd left.

"Somerson really piled it on tonight, didn't she?" Gloria Parks muttered.

"Who cares about homework," Caitlin replied. "I want to hear what you guys think of Jed."

"Not bad at all." Tenny giggled.

"We ought to be asking *you*, Caitlin," Morgan added. "You got all his attention."

Caitlin brought her thoughts back to the present and laughed. "Did I? I hadn't even noticed," she said coyly.

"At least Roger's got some competition now," Jessica Stark, a usually quiet redhead, remarked. "He was really getting *unbearable*."

"There's probably a lot more to Roger than meets the eye," Dorothy said in his defense.

"I agree. Roger's not bad. And what do you expect," Caitlin added, "when all he hears is how he's the school star."

The girls started crossing the lawns from the grouping of Highgate classroom buildings toward the dorms. The magnificent grounds of the exclusive boarding school were spread out around them. The ivy-covered walls of the original school building had changed little in the two hundred years since it had been constructed as the manor house for a prosperous plantation. A sweeping carpet of lawn had replaced the tilled fields of the past; and the smaller buildings had been converted into dormitories and staff quarters. The horse stable had been expanded, and several structures had been added—classroom buildings, a gymnasium complete with an indoor pool, tennis and racketball courts—but the architecture of the new buildings blended in well with that of the old.

"Caitlin, isn't that your grandmother's car in the visitors' parking lot?" Morgan pointed toward the graveled parking area off the oak-shaded main drive. A sleek, silver Mercedes sports coupe was gleaming in the sunlight there.

"So it is." Caitlin frowned momentarily. "Wonder what she's doing here? I must have left something at the house last time I was home for the weekend."

"My dream car!" Gloria exclaimed, holding one hand up to adjust her glasses. "I've told Daddy he absolutely *must* buy me one for my sixteenth birthday."

"And what did he say?" Jessica asked.

Gloria made a face. "That I had to settle for his three-year-old Datsun or get a bicycle."

"Beats walking," Morgan said, reaching into he bag for another candy bar.

"But I'm dying to have a car like your grand mother's."

"It's not bad." Caitlin glanced up at the car. "Sh has the Bentley, too, but this is the car she uses wher she wants to drive herself instead of being chauf feured."

"Think she'll let you bring it here for your senio year?"

Caitlin shrugged and mimicked her grandmother' cultured tones. "'It's not wise to spoil one.' Besides I've always preferred Jaguars."

Caitlin paused on the brick path, and the other girl stopped beside her. "You know, I really should go sa hello to my grandmother. She's probably waiting fo me." She turned quickly to the others. "We've go to have a meeting for this fundraiser. How abou tonight—my room, at seven?"

"Sure."

"Great."

"Darn, I've got to study for an exam tomorrow, Jessica grumbled, "but let me know what yo decide."

"Me, too," Kim commented. "I was on the court all afternoon yesterday practicing for Sunday's tenni tournament and really got behind with m studying."

"Okay, we'll fill you guys in, but make sure yo come to the next meeting. And I don't want an excuses. If you miss the meeting, you're out!" Caitli stressed firmly. "I'll catch the rest of you later, then.

All the girls walked away except Dorothy, wh lingered behind. Just then, a tall, elegantly dressed silver-haired woman walked briskly down the stair from the administrative office in the main schoo building. She moved directly toward the Mercedes quickly opened the driver's door, and slid in behin the wheel.

Caitlin's arm shot up in greeting, but Regina Ryar

ever glanced her way. Instead, she started the ngine and immediately swung out of the parking rea and down the curving drive.

For an instant Caitlin stopped in her tracks. Then vith a wide, carefree smile, she turned back to)orothy and laughed. "I just remembered. She called ast night and said she was dropping off my allow- nce money but would be in a hurry and couldn't tay. My memory really *is* bad. I'll run over and pick it p now."

As Caitlin turned, Dorothy lightly grabbed Caitlin's lbow and spoke softly. "I know you're in a hurry, but an I talk to you for a second, Caitlin? Did you mean vhat you said about Roger? Was he really looking at ne?"

"I told you he was," Caitlin said impatiently, nxious to get Dorothy out of the picture. "Would I lie o you?"

"Oh, no. It's just that when I went over to talk to im, he didn't seem that interested. He was more nterested in listening to what you and Jed were aying."

"Roger's just nosy."

"Well, I wondered. You know, I haven't had any lates since I transferred—"

"Dorothy! You're worried about dates? Are you razy?" Caitlin grinned broadly. "And as far as Roger ;oes, wait and see. Believe me." She gave a breezy vave. "I've got to go."

"Yeah, okay. And, thanks, Caitlin."

"Anytime."

Without a backward glance, Caitlin walked quickly o the administration office. The story about her llowance had been a fabrication. Regina Ryan had ;iven Caitlin more than enough spending money vhen she'd been home two weeks earlier, but it vould be all over campus in a minute if the girls hought there was anything marring Caitlin's seem- ngly perfect life.

Running up the steps and across the main marble-

floored lobby that had once been the elegant entranc
hall of the plantation house, she walked quickly int
the dean's office and smiled warmly at Mrs. Forbe
the dean's secretary.

"Hi, Mrs. Forbes."

"Hello, Caitlin. Can I help you?"

"I came to pick up the message my grandmoth
just left."

"Message?" Mrs. Forbes frowned.

"Yes." Caitlin continued to look cheerful. "I ju
saw her leaving and figured she was in a hurry an
left a message for me here."

"No, she just met on some school board busines
briefly with Dean Fleming."

"She didn't leave anything for me?"

"I can check with the part-time girl if you like.

"Thanks." Caitlin's smile had faded, but she waite
as Mrs. Forbes stepped into a small room at the rea

She returned in a second, shaking her hea
"Sorry, Caitlin."

Caitlin forced herself to smile. "No problem, Mr
Forbes. It wasn't important, anyway. She'll probabl
be on the phone with me ten times tonight."

As Caitlin hurried from the main building and se
out again toward the dorm, her beautiful face wa
grim. Why was she always trying to fool herself? Sh
knew there was no chance her grandmother woul
call just to say hello. But nobody would ever know
that: She would make certain of it. Not Mrs. Forbe
or any of the kids; not even her roommate, Ginn
Not anyone!

Like it so far? Want to read more? LOVING will b
available in May 1985.* It will be on sale wherev
Bantam paperbacks are sold. The other two books i
the trilogy, LOVE DENIED and TRUE LOVE, wi
also be published in 1985.

*Outside the United States and Canada, books will be availab
approximately three months later. Check with your local booksell
for further details.

☐	25033	**DOUBLE LOVE #1**	**$2.50**
☐	25044	**SECRETS #2**	**$2.50**
☐	25034	**PLAYING WITH FIRE #3**	**$2.50**
☐	25143	**POWER PLAY #4**	**$2.50**
☐	25043	**ALL NIGHT LONG #5**	**$2.50**
☐	25105	**DANGEROUS LOVE #6**	**$2.50**
☐	25106	**DEAR SISTER #7**	**$2.50**
☐	25092	**HEARTBREAKER #8**	**$2.50**
☐	25026	**RACING HEARTS #9**	**$2.50**
☐	25016	**WRONG KIND OF GIRL #10**	**$2.50**
☐	25046	**TOO GOOD TO BE TRUE #11**	**$2.50**
☐	25035	**WHEN LOVE DIES #12**	**$2.50**
☐	24524	**KIDNAPPED #13**	**$2.25**
☐	24531	**DECEPTIONS #14**	**$2.50**
☐	24582	**PROMISES #15**	**$2.50**
☐	24672	**RAGS TO RICHES #16**	**$2.50**
☐	24723	**LOVE LETTERS #17**	**$2.50**

SPECIAL
MONEY SAVING
OFFER

Now you can have an up-to-date listing of Bantam's hundreds of titles plus take advantage of our unique and exciting bonus book offer. A special offer which gives you the opportunity to purchase a Bantam book for only 50¢. Here's how!

By ordering any five books at the regular price per order, you can also choose any other single book listed (up to a $4.95 value) for just 50¢. Some restrictions do apply, but for further details why not send for Bantam's listing of titles today!

Just send us your name and address plus 50¢ to defray the postage and handling costs.

☐ 24292	IT MUST BE MAGIC #26 Marian Woodruff	$2.25
☐ 22681	TOO YOUNG FOR LOVE #27 Gailanne Maravel	$1.95
☐ 23053	TRUSTING HEARTS #28 Jocelyn Saal	$1.95
☐ 24312	NEVER LOVE A COWBOY #29 Jesse Dukore	$2.25
☐ 24293	LITTLE WHITE LIES #30 Lois I. Fisher	$2.25
☐ 23189	TOO CLOSE FOR COMFORT #31 Debra Spector	$1.95
☐ 24837	DAY DREAMER #32 Janet Quin-Harkin	$2.25
☐ 23283	DEAR AMANDA #33 Rosemary Vernon	$1.95
☐ 23287	COUNTRY GIRL #34 Melinda Pollowitz	$1.95
☐ 24336	FORBIDDEN LOVE #35 Marian Woodruff	$2.25
☐ 24338	SUMMER DREAMS #36 Barbara Conklin	$2.25
☐ 23340	PORTRAIT OF LOVE #37 Jeanette Noble	$1.95
☐ 24331	RUNNING MATES #38 Jocelyn Saal	$2.25
☐ 24340	FIRST LOVE #39 Debra Spector	$2.25
☐ 24315	SECRETS #40 Anna Aaron	$2.25
☐ 24838	THE TRUTH ABOUT ME AND BOBBY V. #41 Janetta Johns	$2.25
☐ 23532	THE PERFECT MATCH #42 Marian Woodruff	$1.95
☐ 23533	TENDER-LOVING-CARE #43 Anne Park	$1.95
☐ 23534	LONG DISTANCE LOVE #44 Jesse Dukore	$1.95
☐ 24341	DREAM PROM #45 Margaret Burman	$2.25
☐ 23697	ON THIN ICE #46 Jocelyn Saal	$1.95
☐ 23743	TE AMO MEANS I LOVE YOU #47 Deborah Kent	$1.95
☐ 24688	SECRET ADMIRER #81 Debra Spector	$2.25
☐ 24383	HEY, GOOD LOOKING #82 Jane Polcovar	$2.25

Prices and availability subject to change without notice.